D1059911

A THING OF THE PAST

Something was wrong, in and around London. Men were not shaving; women were becoming slipshod, dowdy and sullen-faced. People were bad-tempered, lacking self respect, and crime was on the increase. And, linked to these strange evidences of atavism, was a one-time excavation site. Now a mighty smoking crater, it looked as though a meteorite had descended . . . and from the vast fissure below the crater, there emerged the hideous survivors of a lost age of monster dinosaurs . . .

JOHN RUSSELL FEARN

A THING OF THE PAST

Complete and Unabridged

LINFORD
Leicester

First published in Great Britain

First Linford Edition
published 2010

British Library CIP Data

Fearn, John Russell, *1908 – 1960.*
 A thing of the past. - -
 (Linford mystery library)
 1. Science fiction.
 2. Large type books.
 I. Title II. Series
 823.9'12–dc22

ISBN 978–1–44480–456–0

Published by
F. A. Thorpe (Publishing)
Anstey, Leicestershire

Set by Words & Graphics Ltd.
Anstey, Leicestershire
Printed and bound in Great Britain by
T. J. International Ltd., Padstow, Cornwall

This book is printed on acid-free paper

1

The fissure

The monstrous face of the basalt cliff lifted outwards under the impact of the explosion. Rocks and subsoil flew. Small boulders flashed to the zenith and rained down amidst a cloud of choking dust. On the hot summer wind a rumbling died away into silence and all was quiet.

'That seems to be it, Mr. Brooks,' the field engineer said, cuffing up his steel helmet and mopping his face. 'That's the last of 'em. Clearance is complete, or will be when the mechanical navvies have finished.'

Clifford Brooks nodded. He was the mining engineer in charge of the whole operation. For six weeks now throughout the unusually hot summer he and his band of iron-hard men had been at work removing a basalt area so that the ever-spreading environs of London could

1

spread even further.

'Better take a look at it, Dick,' he said briefly; 'Make sure everything's as it should be.'

The field engineer nodded and, with Cliff Brooks by his side, he strode across the busy mining area, picking his way amidst the equipment whilst the men lounged around waiting for their next orders.

After a while the two engineers reached the summit of the rubble mountain that the exploded gelignite had ejected. They looked around them in the dust haze. The whole mass of the basalt cliff that had formerly stood in their way was now completely levelled. Once the rubbish was moved there would be a flat area around here many square miles in extent, in prime condition for laying the foundations of a new building scheme.

'Satisfactory enough,' Cliff Brooks said, nodding. He was a tall, rangy man, rather like the popular conception of a Western hero, his skin a burned-in brown, his eyes blue, his face lean-jawed and extremely determined.

'Hear something?' asked the field

engineer after a moment, frowning, his head cocked very slightly.

'Nothing more than usual. Bits of rock dropping, sound of the wind in niches . . . '

'No, no, a sort of buried rumbling. Listen!' The field engineer held up his brown hand urgently, and now Cliff Brooks heard it too. It sounded like a train at the far end of a very long tunnel. Somehow there was something vaguely frightening about it, an odd suggestion of deep, buried power.

'Sounds like thousands of tons of rubbish going down a deep mine,' the field engineer said. 'Where the hell's it coming from, anyway?'

They began moving again, searching around them in the ruin of debris and rocks, then presently they both halted on the edge of a hole. They looked into it, then at each other. The noise was coming from inside the hole. Down there was a shaft, but what its depth was they could not imagine. Standing there on the edge of the hole the noises that came from below sounded a thousand miles away.

'Must be some kind of old fissure,' Cliff

Brooks said finally. 'Certainly not a new one, or a volcanic root, else we'd have had lava and God knows what raining on us by now. Get the boys to bring the tackle. I'm going down to see what it's like. We'll probably have to fill it in.'

The field engineer turned away, and then hurried down the slope to give his orders to the waiting men. Cliff Brooks laid flat and peered into the depths, sniffing at the draught blowing upward. It smelled sweet enough — no mephitic gas of any kind — and it was slightly warm. This latter fact he could well understand since the shaft probably connected with the core of volcanic matter somewhere. That core must be a long way off, though, for here in Britain volcanic areas just did not exist —

Then the brawny, sweating men were coming up the slope in the hot afternoon sunlight bearing with them the ropes, trestles and block and tackle necessary for a descent into the depths. In a very short time they had a cable and harness rigged up, and Cliff made himself comfortable within it.

'Lower away,' he instructed, switching on his torch. 'I'll give the usual signal when I want to come back.'

The field engineer himself took charge of operations, and gradually Cliff found himself descending from the burning sunlight into the warm, dark depths, the draught blowing up past him as he went down. Just at this point the shaft was not very wide; so that his torch beam easily reached the walls on either side. From the appearance of the rock it was plain that the shaft was Nature's handiwork: the explosion had not unexpectedly revealed some earthwork performed by men in the dim past.

The narrow width of the shaft persisted for nearly two hundred feet, then it suddenly branched away, and Cliff found himself swinging in a great abyss from which all signs of walls had gone. His torch beam completely failed to reach them. Up above there was a pinprick of bright light that marked the spot where the hole opened to the surface.

'Everything all, right, Mr. Brooks?' came the field engineer's voice over Cliff's tiny portable radio.

'Okay so far. Keep on lowering me. First time I ever saw a shaft like this. It's opened now into a big cavern — or something. I'm right in empty air at the moment and it's getting colder instead of warmer.'

This was a fact. The warm air was apparently escaping into the narrow part of the shaft, possibly from unseen blowholes in the rocks that connected deeply with the Earth's faraway volcanic depths. Here, in the more open region, the warmth had gone and a glacial coldness was descending. Cliff gave a little shiver as perspiration chilled upon him.

Then suddenly he saw ground coming up to meet him in the torch beam. He landed on his feet without hurt and gave the 'Stay put' pull on the guide rope as he detached himself from the harness. Torch in hand he looked about him, conscious of the intense, sepulchral cold.

He was certainly in some kind of underground cave, great daggers of limestone rock pointing down at him, from high above, except from the black hole through which he had come. Then there was that mysterious rumbling note. He could still hear it, much more forcibly now, but it still seemed be coming from below. Drawn on by the fascinating mystery of the whole thing he explored farther, doing his best to disregard the intense cold.

Just in time he stopped himself as he came to the edge of a sheer cliff. Amazed, he stared over it into incomprehensible depths. It seemed incredible that there could be a gorge so vast in the Earth itself. It went into absolute remoteness, but at a colossal distance below there seemed to be something vaguely white. It had a curious phosphorescent quality, for, though he tried to the limit he could not bring his eyes to focus on this unimaginably faraway phenomenon.

'Okay?' rang out the friendly voice of the field engineer.

'Yes, but frozen stiff. I'm looking at something I don't understand, some kind of gorge that looks as though it opens into the very core of the Earth itself. That can't be right though, else there'd be steam and hellfire coming up. I can see a long slope going down into infinity — Just a moment whilst I try an age-old experiment.'

Turning, Cliff picked up a reasonably heavy boulder, whitish with a glaze of frost. He heaved it into the canyon and then counted the seconds until there should come the sound of the stone arriving, whereby to roughly estimate the distance in feet. But there was no answering sound. As far as he knew the stone never hit bottom, or else the noise of it doing so was lost. The buried, mystic rumbling remained unchanged.

'Deeper than anything man ever encountered before,' he announced into the microphone. 'Have to take a proper look at it later — '

He stopped speaking abruptly, his eye catching sight for the first time of a mighty glacier wall to the rear of him. It looked exactly like green glass. This in itself was remarkable enough, testifying to the extreme cold at this particular region in contrast with the warmth of the higher levels — but even more remarkable was the sight of something white and oval very near the outer surface of the glacier wall. Cliff began moving towards it.

'You all right?' came an anxious enquiry. 'You stopped talking very suddenly.'

'I'm all right, yes: just looking at something odd.'

Cliff ran his fingers over the iron hard smoothness of the glacier wall's face, his torch beam fixed on the oval something. It was shaped rather like an egg. It was an egg!

'I'll be damned,' Cliff muttered; then into the microphone: 'Send down a pickaxe, please, right away. I've happened on to the biggest egg I ever saw. May be interesting to find out what laid it.'

There was an interval whilst the pickaxe was sent down, then Cliff went to work, carefully nicking the ice away in a big circle from around the mystery object. It took him half an hour to get it free so scared was he of breaking it. Then he laid it down in its bed of chipped ice and peered at it again in the torchlight. It measured some eighteen inches from tip to tip, and possibly nine inches across. In colour it was muddy brown-white, but appeared to be in perfect condition thanks to the ice that had preserved it.

'I'm coming up again,' he announced, carefully packing the huge egg into the haversack of small tools and odds and ends he had brought with him. 'Raise me as carefully as you can.'

He held the egg carefully against him as he was lifted up the shaft once more, and by the time he had reached the top the ice around the egg had completely melted, soaking the haversack and his shirt.

'What the blazes laid a thing like that?' the field engineer asked in amazement as Cliff came out of the harness and held the egg up proudly.

'No idea, but I mean to find out by the simple process of hatching it. May have been down there in the ice for centuries.'

'Any idea why there should be ice down there?' the field engineer asked.

'No idea at all, unless it's some kind of drift from an underground glacial region, which is quite possible. Take an expert geologist to work that one out.' Cliff's expression changed slowly as he stood thinking. 'Something very queer down there, boys,' he continued. 'Warm volcanic draughts, ice cold mass of glacier in which I found this, and a gorge of inconceivable depth going down into — Well I just don't know what.'

'The answer to all this being what?' the field engineer asked. 'Can this region be passed as okay for building?'

Cliff shook his head. 'Not yet. For one thing this narrow shaft will have to be thoroughly examined in case there's a chance of a subsidence later into that big cavern I landed in. This whole area's in considerable danger of lunging inwards at some future date. I'm taking no responsibility. If the geologists issue a certificate, then that passes the buck to them. Right now there's nothing more we can do but get this rubbish shovelled up. You look after it, Dick, and I'll go into town and report to headquarters.'

'Okay,' the field engineer promised, and Cliff went on his way still carrying the mystery egg with infinite care. When he

11

arrived home that evening he still had it with him, but by now it was in a cardboard box lined with cotton wool. With a certain air of mystery, like a magician about to perform a trick, he displayed the egg to his wife.

'What is it?' Joan asked, not particularly pleased at having the untidy old box dumped on the spotlessly white table-cloth.

'An egg,' Cliff said proudly. 'The biggest egg you ever saw!'

'I can tell that. What laid it, an ostrich?'

'Heavens, no! An ostrich's egg would be tiny beside this. I'm going to hatch it out and see what comes of it.'

'Oh, I see.' Joan looked rather stupid for a moment. Not because she really was stupid, but because she could not imagine why anybody should wish to bring home an outsize egg and hatch it just for the hell of it.

'I found it in a glacier nearly three hundred feet down in the ground,' Cliff explained, hoping this information would stir up interest. 'Very uncommon happening, I can tell you.'

'Uh-huh — Are you having the remainder of the cold meat or shall I make it up into rissoles?'

'It'll do as it is,' Cliff replied absently. 'Too hot for rissoles, anyway.'

Joan shrugged and wandered off into the kitchen regions. Cliff looked after her and sighed. Joan was a good sort in most things — nice cook, kept the house perfect, only she had very little imagination and relied far too much on gadgets to help her with her work, when a little physical elbow grease might have done her a world of good. Cliff never regretted that he had married her, but he could have wished for a girl slightly quicker on the uptake.

'Be back in a minute,' he called out as crockery rattled in the kitchenette.

'Back? You've only just come in. Where are you going?'

'To put the egg in the garage. Warm enough in there this weather to hatch it.'

'Oh!' Just that: nothing more. By the time Cliff had rid himself of the egg, freshened up and was seated at the table Joan seemed to have forgotten all about

13

the egg until Cliff jogged her memory.

'It's possible,' he said, musing, 'that the egg may have been buried down in that underworld glacier for many hundreds, or even thousands, of years.'

Joan reflected. She was a tired-looking young woman with ash-blonde hair and hazel eyes. Not so bad looking really, only the romance seemed to have gone out of life, and she found married domesticity pretty humdrum. The thought of an egg buried in a glacier for thousands of years was hardly the basis of a pep talk either.

'I've seen the geologists,' Cliff continued. 'They're going to explore the cavern where I found the egg and the shaft that leads down to it — ' and he went on to explain in detail, including an account of the mighty gorge that he had been quite unable to fathom.

'You surely don't suppose,' Joan asked at length, 'that that egg can possibly have anything in it? Not after the hundreds or thousands of years you so cheerfully speak of. Why, it ought to be — be rotten.'

'Not if preserved in ice, dear. That's the

14

whole point. Do you realise that living bacteria, perhaps millions of years old, have been dug out of ice from time to time in circumstances very similar to these?'

'Think of that!' Joan went on with her meal. Eggs did not appeal to her in any case, either for eating purposes or for scientific investigation. In fact, the thought of an egg that size made her feel strangely queasy within. Cliff sensed this fact and slightly changed the subject.

'We got the site flattened out all right at last, thank goodness, but I don't know what's going to be done about that shaft. Maybe have to fill it in. Make foundations rocky if we — '

The front door bell rang. Throwing down his napkin impatiently he headed out of the room, returning with Bill Masterson, the thick-necked, bull-headed geologist of the mining concern.

'Howdy, Joan,' he greeted briefly, and then settled himself in the nearest armchair. 'Don't let me upset feeding time: I just wanted to tell you personally, Cliff, what I think you've run into back at the site.'

Cliff resumed his seat at the table. 'You've examined the shaft then?'

'Certainly, and the cavern below. That explosion you set off to blow out the basalt opened a natural fissure that leads down into a completely preserved Jurassic Period. No doubt of it whatever. Up to now geologists have been content to find a few fragments of some past age — a bit of Triassic, maybe, or a bit of Eocene, but never have we landed on a whole area preserved exactly as it must have been in that period. You have done science a wonderful service, Cliff, and I intend to let the scientists know that.'

'Well, thanks very much. Sheer chance, anyway.' Cliff frowned as he ate his meal. 'How do you mean — perfectly preserved? How could it be?'

'It's like this. At the depth you reached — three hundred feet down — there was once a surface landscape of the Jurassic Period. Then something must have happened. Maybe a gigantic earthquake, or even a general sliding of the Earth's surface. That area was covered with rock, but atmospheric pressures — steam

pressures, that is, from inside the Earth
— formed a gigantic blowhole in the
shape of that cavern. A new surface
formed over the hole and it's lain there
untouched ever since. As the pressures
relaxed and the volcanic heat abated
water vapour would form. Its drops
caused the stalactites to form in the roof.
It was after the Jurassic and Mesozoic
Periods, the age of the dinosaurs, that a
second glacial epoch descended on the
world, and it is possible that that mighty
buried glacier is a part of it, still
unthawed because down in that huge cave
there is so little warmth.'

Silence, save for the clink of knives and
forks.

'How long ago did all this happen?'
Joan asked finally. 'The Jurassic Age, I
mean.'

'Oh, around eighty million years ago.'

Joan smiled weakly and made no
comment. Cliff, though, stopped eating.

'Eighty million years! But that egg I
found just couldn't be — '

'What egg?' Bill Masterson's eyebrows
went up.

'I found an egg in that glacier wall and dug it out. Maybe you noticed the space in the glacier where I'd been busy?'

'Frankly, no, and if I did I didn't take particular heed.' The geologist's face had become grim. 'Where's this egg now?'

'In the garage. I'm hatching it out just to see what's in it.'

'You may be very horrified when you see what is in it. You surely know enough of geological history to realise that the things that existed eighty million years ago were huge and terrifying? The age of the dinosaurs, man!'

'Yes, but — This couldn't be a dinosaur. It's an egg. It can't mean anything more than a bird.'

Bill Masterson sighed. 'For your information, Cliff, the vertebrated animals of the Jurassic Age laid eggs. They did not procreate in the manner of the later, more refined creatures. If you take my advice you'll smash up this egg from the glacier before things get too tough.'

Cliff shook his head. 'I'm too inquisitive to do that. If something horrible turns up I can very soon destroy it. But

I'm certainly going to see that egg hatch.'

'Very well.' The geologist gave a shrug. 'Don't say I didn't warn you.'

'What about that deeper cavern, or canyon, which Cliff found?' Joan enquired, slowly becoming interested. 'Any ideas on that, Bill?'

'I'm afraid not. I think the buried rumbling may be from great internal activity, or it may be the action of a mighty underground ocean.' Bill pondered for a moment. 'Yes, on reflection I think an ocean is the best theory. If it were internal fire there'd definitely be more warmth coming up the gorge than there is.'

'An underground ocean seems to suggest a whole world within the World,' Cliff said.

'Is that so impossible? If part of the Jurassic Age could be buried, so might a great deal more of it, or even parts of other Ages. I can't help wishing with all my heart that that shaft had never been opened by the explosion, Cliff.'

Cliff grinned. 'It was just one of those things, and I'll be hanged if I see what you're bothered about. Putting aside the scientific issue for the moment, what do we do with the site? Fill it in?'

'Yes.' Masterson got to his feet. 'As quickly as possible, too. Just in case there might be a volcanic upsurge that would blow half of England off the map. You don't seem to realise that you've opened up a vent in this old planet of ours. The effect is not seen immediately, but it may cause a redistribution of internal pressures, and then anything could happen. Yes, get the shaft blocked as fast as possible. Concrete and liquid iron. That should hold things.'

'And what about the scientists? They'll want to have a look at this geologic masterpiece, won't they?'

'They can do it within the next week; you won't have filled the shaft in by then — ' Masterson glanced at his watch. 'Well, I've got to be going, but I thought you'd like the facts before I turn in the official report. I'll tip off the scientists to come and have a look if you like.'

Cliff nodded. 'Do that. Tomorrow I'll have the boys start the sealing process.'

On that the geologist departed, and

Cliff stood thinking, gazing through the wide-open window towards the garage at the bottom of the garden.

'You thinking what I'm thinking?' Joan asked him, drifting to his side.

'I don't know. It just crossed my mind that I'm sticking to that egg, no matter what. I can't see what Bill's getting goose pimples about. If there's anything queer in the egg it can be put to sleep instantly.'

'No guarantee it will even hatch.'

With a mutual thought in their minds and their meal over they strolled out through the kitchenette door into the garden. The evening was hot and misty with a promise of thunder to come. These were everyday phenomena, though. In the garage there was a thing of the past, and down under the Earth there was also a region upon which man had never set eyes for eighty million years until Cliff had descended the shaft.

'No harm in seeing how the egg's going on,' he said as he and Joan reached the garage doors.

'No harm at all. That's why we're out here, isn't it?'

Cliff opened the doors and looked on the floor at the rear of his two-seater car. The egg was in the cardboard box as he had left it, the lid removed. Nothing had happened yet, anyway.

'Perhaps not warm enough,' Joan said.

'I think it's just right, dear. The period from which this egg came, far as I can remember, was mild and humid — much as it is tonight. The conditions are quite favourable. Don't forget it has to thaw out from the glacier as well.'

Joan stooped and sniffed at the shell. 'Doesn't smell at all, does it?'

'No reason why it should. It was probably quite fresh when the ice or whatever it was caught up. We'll leave it for a day or two and see what happens.'

For an instant it was in Cliff's mind to put his foot into the egg there and then, so strongly did Bill Masterson's sombre warning cross his memory; then he shook his head to himself and closed the garage doors adamantly. He turned to find Joan looking into the misty sky. The sun was hidden in the heat haze low down on the horizon, so it was no effort to stare at the heavens for a prolonged period.

'What is it?' Cliff asked, expecting to see some aerobatics by a jet plane.

'That! I'm trying to make out what it is. Some sort of noiseless plane, isn't it? I've heard that there is one on the secret list — '

Cliff looked long and earnestly, and at last he found the object that Joan's sharper eyes had already detected. It was circling at a height of perhaps three hundred feet, making no sound whatever. Occasionally it dived; then it climbed again with the velocity of an anti-aircraft shell. In some ways it looked like an airplane. In other ways it looked like a bird — Bird? Impossible! There couldn't be a bird of that size, not even the biggest eagle ever known. Why, at close quarters it must be gigantic. It was large enough even seen from three hundred feet below.

'What in the world is it?' Joan demanded at last. For answer Cliff fled into the house and returned after a moment or two with powerful field glasses. Quickly he focussed them as he stared aloft.

'For the love of heaven!' he gasped. 'It's

— it's a pterodactyl! A flying lizard!'

'Huh?' Joan looked blankly at his startled face; then he thrust the glasses into her hands.

'Look for yourself! You've seen drawings of pterodactyls as much as I have. If that isn't one I'm crazy!'

Joan looked, only to confirm Cliff's opinion. The flying horror was partly like a bat, partly like a lizard and having a gun-grey body of apparently tremendous toughness. At a rough estimate Joan guessed the wingspan to be about eighty feet. It kept on circling steadily as if searching for some thing — or else sighting some object or other with its intensely keen eyes.

'It's crazy, but it's right,' Joan exclaimed, lowering the glasses. 'Or *is* it right? Maybe it's some kid's toy kite shaped like a monster. You know how the youngsters play around with scientific things these days — '

'No use kidding ourselves, Joan; it's a pterodactyl. And there's only one place where it could have come from, and that is the shaft of the mining site. Being a bird it could easily fly from its underground prison.'

'But you didn't see anything alive down there, did you?'

'No, but according to Bill Masterson a Jurassic cavern or something has been opened, and there could have been life in that deeper canyon which I didn't explore. Fact remains that that object up there couldn't have come from anywhere else.'

They stood watching it for a time as its gyrations grew gradually less, until finally it seemed to be hovering far above, motionless.

'What's it looking for, do you think?' Joan's eyes were commencing to ache with the constant effort of staring aloft.

'I'm not sure, but I can hazard an uneasy guess. Right in this garage we have something prehistoric, and by some telepathic link, such as does exist among many birds and animals, that flying horror may be aware that an object of its own time and kin is down here.'

'Sort of inverted homing instinct, or something?'

'Like that — yes.' Cliff had the field

glasses still to his eyes — then suddenly he let out a gasp.

'It's diving!' Joan cried at the same moment. 'Quickly! Into the house!'

With appalling swiftness the pterodactyl suddenly began a power dive, swooping with incredible speed from the misty eights, straight down towards the garden. Tripping and tumbling, Cliff and Joan blundered towards the house, gained the kitchenette and slammed the door. Then at top speed they raced into the adjoining living room and watched through the window. Spellbound they watched a scene that had certainly never been viewed before by modern beings.

The pterodactyl had reached the garden, and its size was apparent now as its great wings, dry and membranous, overspread the width of the lawn and became partly entangled with the parting fences on either side. It had a body as big as a man's, yet a head like a vulture on an enormous scale. It was quite the vilest thing ever, its tremendously strong beak pecking and lashing at the strong garage doors.

'I — I feel sort of sick,' Joan whispered, white-faced. 'What in the world do we do now?'

'Nothing,' Cliff snapped. 'That thing's carnivorous, and unlike the modern bird it has triple rows of shark teeth. I just caught a glimpse of them. If we try and deal with that thing we'll be ripped to pieces. It's after that damned egg, sure as fate.'

'Call the police,' Joan urged. 'They'll do something.'

'Not on your life! The police might as well try and fight a tank as fight this. Leave it alone and watch what happens.'

Apparently the terrifying creature was becoming annoyed at finding the garage doors too tough for its onslaught. With a series of ear-splitting screams it flung itself in leathery fury against the barrier, its vast beak tearing great shards and splinters out of the woodwork — but the doors held, and at last the pterodactyl seemed to realise it was beaten. It withdrew and folded its wings, standing for a moment in the centre of the lawn like a colossal bat, its evil head turning slowly until a lidless, deep red eye became visible to the crouching two in the lounge.

'The size of it!' Joan panted. 'I'd say it's nearly twenty feet high!'

'Nearer thirty — Ah! Thank God for that!'

The flying lizard had suddenly spread its wings again and, with another piercing, unearthly scream, it took off into the evening mist and was gradually lost to sight. The only trace of it ever having been present at all lay in the battered garage doors and huge three-claw imprints in the soft soil of the flowerbeds. It had been no nightmare then. The past had come into the present and there was no foreseeing the repercussions.

2

Flying lizard

After a few moments the quiet suburban region in which Cliff and Joan lived seemed suddenly to come to life again. Neighbours from both sides appeared over the fence and asked an endless stream of questions. Down the road from houses nearby came men and women, likewise interrogative. The descent of the pterodactyl had been seen by nearly everybody in the vicinity and, wisely, nobody had attempted to investigate until the horror had flown away.

Mr. Biltmore, Cliff's right-hand neighbour, went further than just shouting questions over the fence. He climbed the fence itself and came into the lounge.

'For hell's sake, Mr. Brooks, what was that thing?' he demanded. 'I never saw anything like it.'

'Pterodactyl,' Cliff answered briefly.

'Damnably dangerous, too. Excuse me, will you, I've an urgent phone call to make.'

'Sure thing. What did you make of it, Mrs. Brooks?' Cliff left Joan to handle the enquiries and went to the phone in the hall, ignoring the incessant ringing of the front door bell by other equally mystified neighbours.

'Bill?' Cliff asked urgently after a while. 'Cliff here. We've got to act fast on that shaft and I'll need your help, of course, on the geologic side.'

'Naturally,' Bill Masterson agreed, sounding somewhat surprised. 'I thought you said tomorrow — '

'Tomorrow won't do. That shaft has got to be sealed — at least temporarily — tonight. I gather you don't know anything about the pterodactyl?'

'The *what*?'

Cliff gave the details briefly, and from the other end there came a whistle.

'That's bad, Cliff — damned bad. Maybe that whole underground area is infested with Jurassic life which is escaping up the shaft.'

'That's what I'm afraid of. Only the birds can get out at the moment, and they must be stopped. We'd better get over to the site right away. I'll tip off my field engineer to get the boys together.'

Things moved fast thereafter — as did the news of the pterodactyl. Joan was left to satisfy wondering neighbours and an hour after Cliff's departure to the basalt site she also had the London newspaper reporters and photographers to deal with. She worked harder than she had ever done in her life, and by eleven-thirty had a lounge full of wondering, curious people, whilst in the garden flashlights were exploding brightly as the damaged garage was photographed. At eleven forty-five came the police who very solemnly took down the particulars. It was perfectly obvious they didn't know what they were dealing with, and more than one began to suspect Joan was just a hysterical woman who had somehow been frightened by an extra large bat on a nocturnal excursion into the summer night.

'It was *not* a bat!' Joan cried, hot and

bothered. 'It was a pterodactyl — a thing of the past. Huge!' She spread her arms expressively. 'It attacked the garage.'

'Why?' asked a police sergeant heavily.

'Because — ' Joan stopped. She was loyal to the egg now, as her husband was. 'Because it took a fancy to it. Don't ask me why — Let me have a bit of peace, can't you? All the rest of these neighbours of mine saw the bird, so don't blame it all on to me!'

With this she retired from the fight, vaguely wondering why her husband could not pursue a job that would not necessitate him releasing something from the past. Cliff, for his part, was almost of the same frame of mind when he, Bill Masterson and the entire gang of mining engineers arrived at the basalt site shortly after midnight. The night watchman in charge of the equipment looked as though he had never been so glad to see human beings before. 'It's a miracle you've come as you have!' he exclaimed as the men gathered around him in the light of the safety lamps. 'I've been at my wits' end to know what to do — whether to leave here and get help, or stick it out and trust to luck.'

'Meaning what?' Cliff asked briefly.

'Why, the shaft! Things keep comin' out of there that are the invention of Old Nick himself! Birds as big as houses — must have been dozens of 'em!'

Bill Masterson gripped the old man's arm. 'Dozens? Did you say *dozens?* Be absolutely sure about this. It's mighty important.'

'Well, I didn't exactly count 'em one by one, Mr. Masterson, but I'm darned sure there was thirty or forty. The things've been flying outa the shaft ever since nightfall.'

'That's lovely,' Cliff muttered. 'Thirty or forty pterodactyls on the loose! Let's take a look at that shaft and see what we can do to block it up.'

He jerked his head to Masterson, the field engineer, and the rest of the men. Leaving the watchman muttering to himself about goblins and inventions of the Devil they made their way across the site, the field engineer switching on the full battery of arc lamps as they went. By the time they had gained the position of the shaft the area of debris was lighted as though by sunshine.

'Nothing different about the hole anyhow,' Masterson said. 'We ought to be thankful that only birds can get up from below. If there are other things they'd have broken loose too, and a nice mess we'd have been in.'

'I'm not so frightfully happy at the thought of forty odd lizards doing as they like,' Cliff commented. 'And the more I look at this shaft the more I think we'll just waste our time trying to temporarily block it up. The better way would be to destroy it completely.'

'How?' the field engineer questioned.

'Load the sides of the shafts with gelignite and blow the whole issue out of existence. It will make a big subsidence on the surface here, of course, but at least it will seal the underworld up for good.'

'Technically,' Masterson said, thinking, 'it's sane enough but I hate the thought of throwing away a perfectly preserved Jurassic region before even the scientists have had a chance to look at it.'

'When it's a toss-up between the scientists and flying lizards I know which my money is on!' Cliff turned to the field engineer. 'We'll get the shaft loaded, Dick. It's the only course. Get the stuff.'

'Okay.'

There was silence between Masterson and Cliff for a while as the required equipment was moved into place, then the geologist asked a question.

'What happens if, when one of the boys is loading the shaft, a pterodactyl comes up from below? He'll be killed, you know.'

'I know. I'm doing the job myself to save calling for a volunteer.'

To which there was nothing more to be said. Cliff rid himself of his leather jacket and then settled into the harness as the men got it into position. With the explosive sticks in a satchel about his shoulders and the shaft brilliantly lighted by a down-turned searchlight he began the descent, giving the stop order when he was half way. Then began work with the small electric drill. It occurred to him once or twice as he worked that he was coughing a good deal, a most unusual thing for him, and presently he thought he knew the reason why.

There was some kind of gas coming up the shaft, where formerly the air had been pure. Possibly by creating a continuous draught through the shaft a good deal of mephitic air had been sucked upwards. Whatever the cause it did not interest him any longer: his main aim was to get the shaft destroyed and be done with the whole alarming business.

All the time he worked and coughed he kept a wary eye on the depths below, but there were no signs of a winged horror speeding upwards to spell his doom. Perhaps all of them had escaped by now.

Altogether he set six charges, three in each side of the shaft, and then he gave the order to haul away. Perspiring freely and half choked he reached the surface and dragged the harness away from him. Then he handed the wiring reels carefully to the field engineer, and the whole party retreated to a safe distance. Connections were made, the plunger driven home, and then it seemed that all hell broke loose.

The men were prepared for a violent

explosion, but not for the livid sheet of orange flame that came with the detonation itself. Blasts of hot air overturned the equipment, boulders were flung through the glare of artificial lighting, the whole area of the shaft gulped and heaved and then settled down into a rumbling avalanche of subsidence. Slowly the din and confusion died away and a dense pall of dust and smoke was left behind.

'That was a tough one,' Masterson commented at length, raising his steel-helmeted head. 'What the blazes happened?'

'There was gas in that shaft,' Cliff told him. 'It must have been volatile and ignited with the explosion. From the look of things we've sealed the spot up, anyway. Let's take a look.'

They returned quickly through the smoke wreaths, the men straightening the fallen lamps as they went. When at length the position of the shaft opening was gained there was nothing visible except smashed and blackened rock caved down into a deep subsidence.

'That's that,' Masterson said in relief. 'The scientists won't be at all pleased after my inviting them to come take a look, but that can't be helped. Maybe the pterodactyls will console them if they're still not captured.'

Cliff nodded. 'Tomorrow we'll start levelling this lot off and take soundings to see how deep this rock covering goes. A warning must also be issued against sinking any deep wells or extra deep foundation. Now let's get out. We've done enough for one night.'

It was well into the early hours when Clifford returned home again, to discover that the various enquiries concerning the pterodactyl had ceased with the departure of the mob. Joan was half-asleep in an armchair, waiting up for him.

'Well?' She hid a yawn behind her hand. 'How did it go?'

'Very well. We sealed the shaft and that puts an end to the Jurassic trouble. The only thing I don't like is the thought of forty odd pterodactyls flying about the landscape.'

'What! Forty of those horrors?'

'According to our watchman, yes. He's a bit of a Mary Ann though, and probably counted a shadow with each one. Just the same I've got to inform the authorities. You get off to bed, dear. You're worn out.'

Joan did not need telling twice. Cliff went into the hall to the telephone and contacted the night division of Scotland Yard. It took him a long time to make matters clear to the inspector in charge. Pterodactyls were not exactly in his line.

'These creatures are dangerous,' Cliff explained laboriously. 'They're seven or eight times bigger than the golden eagle and carnivorous. Inform all police departments to have their men on the lookout for these flying horrors. When they are sighted their point of alighting should be carefully noted. After that it will be up to the Army to destroy them. Nothing less than a three-inch shell can guarantee their destruction.'

'What are they made of? Iron?' the inspector asked dourly.

'Very hard crustacean-shell covering. Ordinary bullets will glance off that.'

'I see. And your name is — what, sir?'

'Clifford Brooks. I've told you three times already.'

'Yes, sir. And thank you. Goodnight.'

The line clicked, and whilst Cliff wondered if the story he had related had been understood the inspector at the other end sighed and shook his head.

'What will these drunks think of next?' he muttered, throwing the notes he had made into the wastepaper basket. 'Flying lizards! Anyway it's a change from pink elephants.'

Cliff went to bed in a most uncertain frame of mind, nor did he sleep well either. The memory of the evening pterodactyl was too strong in his memory for one thing, and his nerve-racking job in the shaft still kept recurring to him. He lay awake and wondered — wondered about the flying lizards which were now probably drifting around the darkened countryside, wondered about the egg in the cardboard box, and wondered about the weird fragment of the Jurassic Age which was now sealed up.

He must have fallen asleep towards dawn, for when he awoke it was half past nine, two hours past his usual time. There was a smell of bacon and coffee in the air, and sunlight poured through the window.

'Blast!' he muttered as he saw the alarm clock. 'Two hours behind and the alarm didn't go off — ' He scrambled out of bed and dragged on his dressing gown. 'Hey, Joan, why didn't you wake me? Look at the time! I'm due on the site at nine.'

'Let them wait! You can't work all night and all day too. Not whilst I'm your wife, anyway. I stopped the alarm — Come on down. The breakfast's good and the news is terrific.'

Cliff wasted no more time. In ten minutes flat he was shaved and dressed. The first thing that greeted him at the breakfast table was the morning paper's headlines:

FLYING LIZARD ATTACKS GARAGE!

The account that followed was not particularly well written, probably because the reporter concerned was not at all sure of his subject. Indeed, parts of the report sounded almost comical. A bat-like object as large as a bell-tent had attacked a private garage and damaged the doors. Some said they did not know what the flying horror really was, others declared it was a pterodactyl. Here there followed an asterisk and a brief notation: 'Pterodactyl — an extinct bird which existed forty million years ago before income tax was even thought of.'

'Very funny,' Cliff commented sourly, throwing the paper down. 'The genius who wrote that is going to think differently if those steel-trap jaws should close around his neck. Whouf! And he'd be decapitated!'

'No mention of the other birds,' Joan said, handing over the bacon and egg. 'Maybe the watchman dreamed it.'

'Maybe, though I don't think he's that big a mug. The likely answer is that the creatures settled somewhere during the dark hours and will get on the move by daylight. Far as I remember they are diurnal, not nocturnal.'

Joan nodded vaguely, wondering what the difference was. She poured out the coffee and studied Cliff's troubled face.

'Don't let it worry you, Cliff. What are a few birds, anyhow? Even if they are big and armour-plated, we've got weapons to blow them to bits. We can always use atom bombs if all else fails.'

Cliff grinned faintly. 'Bless you! One hardly needs to go to the length of using an atom bomb. An ordinary shell, well placed, will put paid to any pterodactyl. What's worrying me is that we just had to seal up that shaft. It would have been a wonderful chance to check up on pre-history if things hadn't proved so dangerous.'

'Seems to me that pre-history doesn't matter much. It's the future which counts.'

Cliff gave it up. It was little use trying to impress on Joan the wonderful scientific issues of the situation: she just was not made that way, and even the close encounter with the pterodactyl the evening before had not in any way changed her.

'Be home for lunch?' she asked presently.

'No idea.' Cliff got up hastily. 'Depends how much I have to look after at the site. I'll give you a ring later. Now I've got to dash.'

He was out of the house and into his car in a matter of three minutes, and it was the fact that he nearly drove the car over the box containing the glacial egg that drew Joan's attention to it. He was far too hurried at the moment to do any examining — but she wasn't. Thoughtfully she crossed the garden, gave a glance at the three-toed impressions from the evening before, and then she looked down at the egg.

She did not know whether it was coincidence or the heat of the sun shining straight down on the box — but at the very moment she contemplated it the shell suddenly cracked and a most incredible little head peeped forth.

'Oh!' Joan gasped, wide-eyed; then as it dawned upon her that the new arrival in this world of cares was not so horrible after all, she continued to gaze at it. It reminded her of a large bird, all eyes and tight-skinned skull of a metal-grey colour. And the creature was plainly hungry, for its mouth opened wide at intervals.

'You poor little thing,' Joan murmured, and feeling very proud of her courage she carried the entire box into the kitchenette and began feeding operations with a bottle of milk, to the neck of which she attached the finger of a rubber glove. The appetite of the creature was prodigious, and the more milk it had the more vigorous it became, until at length it had broken entirely free of the shell and lay in the little bed of cotton-wool which Joan had prepared for it inside the box. Her interest in the unknown thing was genuine: she felt really sorry for it, born some forty million years behind time!

Meanwhile, reports were drifting into various police headquarters up and down the country concerning gigantic birds which had raided chicken runs, attacked cattle, and in some cases, carried away screaming pigs. One report of this nature could have been forgivably discredited, but not half a dozen from different parts of the country. Policemen were sent out to look into the matter — most of them village policemen, too, and their knowledge of monsters from the Jurassic Age could hardly be styled profound. Notes were taken, doubting eyes studied huge three-toe marks in soft soil, and an empty summer sky was contemplated.

At Scotland Yard these reports were known, but the night inspector who was now off duty could not be contacted, though in the checking room it was known he had received warning reports and done no more about it. There were grim faces amongst the high-ups. That inspector was due for heavy censure. The matter of the flying lizards was gradually becoming a matter of national importance.

It became so at half past eleven that morning. Farmer Nathaniel Hurley made history that morning, though probably he would much have preferred not to. The fact was that upon leaving one of the cowsheds he saw a pterodactyl coming straight for him — or else the cows in the shed he had left. He did not have time to classify the winged horror with the scarlet eyes and yawning jaws: he simply whipped up a hayfork and drove it straight into the hurtling creature's face.

Farmer Hurley was not a particularly brave man. It just happened that three things combined in his favour at the identical moment — a hayfork, a powerful arm, and a deadly blow to a vital spot. The winged horror dropped, the fork driven clean through its brain. In a matter of ten seconds it was a quivering, leathery mass, twitching in after-death reaction.

Farmer Hurley afterwards drove three miles to the nearest town and reported his adventure to the police. Once again Scotland Yard was advised, and towards noon an inspector called on Joan as she was in the midst of preparing lunch.

'My apologies for troubling you, Mrs. Brooks,' the inspector said politely. 'It is your husband I'm seeking. Where can I find him?' Joan raised an eyebrow.

'We wish to have details of strange prehistoric birds about which he telephoned to the Yard last night. The message was not — er — complete, and I want first-hand facts. There's a lot of trouble going on up and down the country and we may have to bring in the Army to settle it.'

'Oh — I see.' Joan pulled bits of harden-ing pastry from her forearms. 'You'll find him at what's called the 'basalt site'. Better still, if you go to the Mining Engineers headquarters in Great Union Street they'll be able to run you out to the spot. I hardly know myself how to get there.'

'Thank you, Mrs. Brooks, and my apologies again — Oh, I would suggest you exercise caution whenever you are out of doors. We are giving that advice to everybody on the radio and television. I gather your home has already been once attacked by a pterodactyl?'

'Last night,' Joan agreed. 'That was probably because of Herbert.'

'Herbert?'

'Er — just a joke,' Joan said lamely, at which the inspector gave a dubious glance and then went on his way. Closing the door upon him Joan reflected it might have been difficult to explain that 'Herbert' was a loveable little creature just hatched from a forty-million-year-old egg.

And, unaware of the prehistoric depredations going on up and down the country, Cliff was not having a particularly happy time at the basalt site. The field engineer who was in charge of the original soundings had an unpleasant warning to give, and he gave it after two hours of careful testing in order to be sure of his facts.

'In my view, Mr. Brooks, there's a hell of a lot trouble coming,' he announced as he, Cliff and Bill Masterson held a conference in the site office. 'Our detectors are showing a tremendous pressure pocket in the spot where you blew up that shaft.'

'That's only normal, isn't it?' Bill Masterson demanded. 'All the air which was formerly escaping in the form of draught is now — '

'This isn't air, Mr. Masterson, it's gas. There's no doubt about it. We've had our sounding drills down for three hundred feet, and their test ampoules are loaded with gas when they come up. Queer sort of gas it seems to be: I've got our analysts at work on it now.'

'It's irritant gas of some kind,' Cliff explained. 'I noticed it last night when I was at work in the shaft. Gave me several bad coughing bouts. I'd say it's volcanic in origin.'

'More than likely.' The field engineer gave a grim nod. 'And you know what that means! Before we're much older that sunken shaft is likely to blow its top!'

Masterson and Cliff frowned at each other.

'Why?' Cliff demanded. 'Before we uncovered that blowhole there was no trouble. There's probably been gas pressure down there for millions of years. Forty million that we can almost be sure of, eh, Bill?'

'Definitely,' Masterson conceded.

'There was no trace of gas down there when you descended the first time yesterday, was there, Cliff?' the field engineer questioned.

'No. I noticed how sweet the air was.'

'Then it seems to me that this mysterious gas has escaped since! We don't know whether it was our initial explosion which opened up that giant canyon below, or whether it has always been like that — but I'll lay even money that the gas is coming from there, and sooner or later there'll be need for the gas to escape.'

'Perhaps,' Cliff said slowly, 'that deep rumbling I could hear in the depths was volcanic power, or maybe a huge shifting of rocks and underground matter from which the gas has come.'

'Maybe.' The field engineer gave a grim glance at each man. 'Fact remains, boys, we've got to let that gas out before it blows the lid off everything around here.'

'Okay. We can drive in vent tubes to draw it off.' Cliff motioned briefly. 'Better put the work in hand right away, Dick.'

The field engineer nodded and left the office. Bill Masterson stood thinking, his expression troubled.

'Done the best thing, haven't we?' Cliff asked him. 'After all, we dare not reopen the entire shaft without risking another flock of pterodactyls. Vents will keep the pressure within bounds and avoid an explosion. Soon as the gas has been drawn off we'll be all right.'

'We will if the gas ever comes to an end. If it's volcanic, and apparently it is, it may keep on emanating almost constantly. I begin to think we can wipe off this basalt area as a practicable proposition. Certainly we can't build on it with any security, and the conditions near to it are obviously dangerous.'

The door opened and the top man in the site's analytical department came in.

'Seen Dick?' he questioned.

'If it's about that gas you can tell me,' Cliff said.

'Okay, Mr. Brooks. Here are our findings. It's pure nitrogene.'

'Do you mean nitrogen?' Masterson questioned.

'No, I mean nitrogene. Basically it is volcanic, and there have been traces of it in the poisonous vapours emitted by Vesuvius and sundry other volcanoes when in eruption. Chemistry calls it nitrogene because it has traces of nitrogen in it whilst the rest is poison. It combines readily with other atmospheric gases and does not cause explosions in the process of combination.'

'Then that's all right,' Cliff said in relief.

'In that direction, yes,' the chemist agreed, 'but there is another matter we're not so sure about. This gas when tested on rabbits produces a surprising effect. You couldn't find anything much more docile than a rabbit, yet after inhaling some of this stuff in the pure state two of them attacked each other with the fury of wolves. One got killed and the other badly bitten. You can come and see them if you wish.'

'Never mind,' Cliff said, his eyes hard. 'And thanks for the analysis. I'll tell Dick when he comes back.'

The chemist went out and shut the door. Masterson scratched the back of his beefy neck.

'If anything puts this site out of bounds that report does,' Cliff declared. 'If the gas reacts like that on rabbits, how would it be on human beings?'

'I don't know, Cliff, but don't forget that the rabbits got it in the pure state. When it's mixed with the great preponderance of the atmosphere I doubt if there'd be much effect. You didn't feel like murdering anybody after inhaling it in the shaft, did you?'

'No. Nothing outside the cough. Evidently the normal air mixed with it prevented any serious trouble.'

Masterson was silent, clearly wrestling with some kind of problem. He had not resolved it by the time the field engineer came in with the announcement that the vent tubes had been driven into position.

'How many?' Cliff asked.

'Half a dozen. That should be enough to keep things — '

What the field engineer had intended to say was never known, for at that moment the entire site lifted heavenward under the outward belching of a terrific explosion. The impact smashed windows five miles away, and into the sky there poured a vast mushroom of dirty yellow smoke, grimly reminiscent of an atom bomb discharge. Instruments, men, rocks, buildings — all the lot — were either flattened into the ground or flung hundreds of feet through the air. And within the earth there was a rumbling and growling such as volcanic-free Britain had never known before.

3

The earth-bore

Cliff stirred slowly and then almost as quickly relaxed again as he found that his right arm and leg would not move. He opened his eyes and looked about him. The details of his surroundings were immediately familiar. He was in the bedroom at home. Yes, there was Joan in an armchair nearby, sewing some trifle or other.

'What — what happened?' Cliff croaked, and then he stopped in amazement at the rustiness of his own voice. But it was enough to bring Joan, haggard and big-eyed, to his side.

'Take it easy,' she whispered. 'But thank heaven you've recovered consciousness at last. There were times when we thought you — ' She hesitated and then kissed him gently. 'Never mind that. You're talking again, and that's everything.'

'I still say, what happened?' Cliff wished he did not feel so damnably weary.

'Plenty! But for a Scotland Yard inspector you'd be dead.'

'Oh?' Cliff closed his eyes and wondered where the devil Scotland Yard fitted into the hazy picture.

'He came here to ask for you — about the pterodactyls — and I told him to go to the Mining Engineers' headquarters and they'd direct him to the basalt site. He did that, and he, and several mining executives arrived a few minutes after that terrible explosion. They found a few survivors and got them out. You were nailed down under a beam with a boulder on top of it. Had the rescue not been so quick you'd have died. Even as things are it's been touch and go.'

'When did all this happen, Joan? Today?'

'No — ten days ago. You've been suffering from concussion. You also have three broken ribs, a broken arm and double fracture of the leg.'

'Beautiful. Anything else?'

'Yes. A lot.' Joan gave a curiously uneasy glance about her. 'I'll make you some soup and tell you all about it then.'

She headed for the door. Cliff's voice halted her again.

'How about Bill Masterson? And Dick, my field engineer?'

'I'm sorry you asked me that, Cliff. They were killed instantly, I'm afraid.'

Joan departed and Cliff lay with his eyes closed, slowly putting together the pieces of his shattered life. Ten days! It only seemed like a matter of seconds since the explosion had engulfed him. Lucky to have escaped as he had. The deaths of both Bill and Dick took some assimilating. They'd been good friends, both of them. Yet, somehow, Cliff found he was not so grief-stricken as he had somehow expected. They were dead and that was the end of it. He speculated upon his curious callousness — then Joan came back with the soup and fixed his pillows so he could sit up a little.

'Now, what about it?' he asked quietly. 'And don't look so bothered, dearest. I'm not going to die yet — I'm afraid.'

Joan did not smile. The taut lines were still about her mouth and the shadows under her eyes. She looked like a girl who has forgotten what sleep is like.

'It's not you, I'm afraid for,' she said at length. 'It's everything else. Something's terribly wrong somewhere since that explosion, Cliff, and the scientists — the ones Bill Masterson invited to have a look at the Jurassic region — are trying to find out what it is.'

'Wrong? In what way?'

'Hard to explain. People seem to be different — more ill mannered, less considerate, and there's a tremendous increase in crime. However, to get down to specific things, we now have a rip-roaring volcanic region where the basalt site formerly was. Smoke and fumes are still coming out the crater where the blow-up occurred.'

'Crater!' Cliff gave a start. 'How big?'

'Scientists estimate that it is two miles wide, and there is a general fear of a violent volcanic eruption. So far, that has not happened, and until now nobody has ventured to examine the crater closely because of the poisonous vapours and heat. The explanation of the disaster seems to be that your original blasting of the basalt region touched off a very deep volcanic fissure that was latent in releasing its pent-up gases. When they did finally get beyond pressure point the whole works blew up.'

'Mmmm.' Cliff drank some more soup slowly. 'Just the thing Dick feared — Well, what else?'

'The pterodactyls have all been located and destroyed, but it took the Army to do it, and the birds caused a terrific amount of damage amongst livestock. One had even got as far as America before it met its Waterloo. Inspector Manson had the job in hand, and did it thoroughly. Apparently the man you spoke to at the Yard thought you were a drunk, and made no move, so Manson had a good deal of leeway to make up. So the fear of the pterodactyls is at least over. The Government and Scotland Yard are now busy evacuating all areas likely to be threatened by volcanic eruption.'

'Why so dreary, then?'

'I don't know.' Joan passed a hand over her forehead. 'Just the way I feel these days: just the way everybody feels. A feeling of intense depression — and as for the incivility of everybody, it passes comprehension — ' Joan made an effort and smiled. 'Last of all, there's Herbert. I've kept him out of sight as much as possible in case the neighbours ask too many questions. It's getting to be a job, though. He's growing at a terrific speed.'

'Herbert?' Cliff knitted his brows. 'Now where does *he* come in?'

'He was born on the morning of the explosion. You remember the egg, surely? It hatched, and I've been wet nurse to the strangest little animal I ever saw.'

Cliff's eyes opened a little wider as he remembered, and Joan got to her feet. 'I'll fetch him for you. I'm keeping him in the wash house at the moment. Since it's just out of sight for the neighbours they don't know what's going on.'

Joan hurried out and Cliff finished his soup. It was when Joan returned that he really wondered if he had fully recovered consciousness — for, as held by a length of chain fastened to Joan's hand, there appeared the most ugly beast upon which Cliff had ever gazed.

It was about two feet tall at the moment, with a short, thick neck and a kind of collarette embracing it, which looked like a leather frill. It had the vilest snout and two rudimentary horns instead of eyebrows. In some ways it had a resemblance to a baby rhino; in others it had no resemblance to anything sane or natural. Grey in colour with a thick tail, broad at the root and needle-fine at the tip.

'I'll be damned,' Cliff whispered uneasily, and the tiny red eyes of the creature fixed on him steadily from horny sockets.

'He looks fiercer than he is,' Joan explained, leading him forward. 'Don't you think I've done a good job? I fed him on milk to begin with and then gradually changed to meat, dog biscuits, and fish. He'll eat anything.'

'I can believe it,' Cliff muttered, and studied the ugly face as the creature came nearer. It snuffled constantly in the fashion of a bulldog.

'This is your master, Herbert,' Joan explained, patting the thick neck. 'Say your greetings nicely.'

Long pause. Cliff's eyes met the remorseless red ones, then the snout of the thing curled up weirdly and revealed three rows of deadly sharp teeth. A tongue shot out and began to lick Cliff's free hand with the gentleness of a nutmeg grater.

'Nice boy,' he muttered, patting its head. 'Very nice. Now go away before I get the heebie-jeebies.'

'Yes, you've had quite enough,' Joan agreed, and led the heavy-bodied creature out of the room again. After ten minutes she returned with a look of enquiry.

'Nice pet,' Cliff said, lying back, 'but I don't suppose we'll be able to keep him.'

'Why not? I've heard of folk keeping tigers and even elephants. If they're under control there's no fuss. He *does* grow fast, though. Ten days ago he was no bigger than an ordinary loaf, and now look at him. I think we ought to stick to him, though. Science will probably pay a lot of money for him when he's full-grown. After all, he *is* something from forty million years ago.'

'*Eighty* million, Joan.'

'Well, what's the difference? Nobody can conceive the length of time, anyhow — '

Cliff became silent. The vision of the 'adolescent' creature from the Jurassic Age had shaken him considerably, and his knowledge of prehistoric animals was not complete enough to enable him to identify the creature. Then his speculations were brought to an end by the arrival of Dr. Crawford. It was odd, too, how short-tempered Crawford was. An old friend of the Brookses, outside his profession he was usually the most genial of men. Now it took him all his time to be pleasant.

'Sorry, old man,' Cliff said finally, 'but I'm not lying here because I like doing it, or just to annoy you. It's just the way of things.'

'Perhaps. Perhaps not.' Crawford's eyes were cold. 'If you and a few others I could name would stop playing around with natural forces there'd be less accidents and less demands on hard-working doctors. You're doing all right, and I'll come again when I can. Don't call on me unless it's essential.'

'In your present mood I wouldn't dream of it.' Cliff eyed him sourly. 'What's wrong, man? Nerves? I haven't recovered consciousness above an hour, but at least I hope I'm civil.'

Crawford did not answer. He wrote out a prescription, handed it to Joan, then departed with nothing more than a nod.

'See what I mean?' Joan asked as the front door slammed. 'Everybody's like that all of a sudden. As for crime, it's appalling! Murders galore, and thefts by the hundreds. The police just can't cope with it.'

'For the moment,' Cliff said, 'I'm going to try and sleep. I've had quite enough — '

And sleep he did, almost through the day and most of the night. The following day he was much stronger, and certain ideas were filtering into his active mind, stimulated by what he saw on television newscasts and read in the newspapers. Joan had not been exaggerating when she had said something was wrong somewhere. There had to be a reason for vast numbers of men not taking the trouble to shave themselves. And women, the great majority taking a reasonable pride in their appearance, were apparently no longer interested. They were slipshod, dowdy, sullen-faced.

Added to these strange evidences were scenes of the one time basalt site — now a mighty smoking crater that looked as though a meteorite had descended. A laconic announcer explained that the heat was unabated and that therefore investigation of the crater was impossible. The moment the chance afforded, Dr. Adam Blair, in charge of the situation, would make a detailed report.

'I've got to see this chap Blair,' Cliff told Joan when she had given him his breakfast. 'One or two things on which I can enlighten him, and vice versa. Contact his newspaper will you, dear, and have him come over and see me? Explain how I'm fixed.'

Dr. Blair did not waste any time in complying. He was a tall, elderly man, and from his appearance Cliff expected a genial manner. Instead he found himself dealing with a man every bit as acid as Dr. Crawford had been.

'I thought,' Cliff said, 'that we might discuss this matter reasonably. Since I was the engineer in charge of the basalt site I can probably add to your store of knowledge.'

'Very easily, I should think. As yet we know virtually nothing. And what do you mean, Mr. Brooks, by discussing *reasonably*? I thought that was what we were doing!'

'That's a matter of opinion.' Cliff hesitated, wondering whether to give the scientist the brush off or not; then he decided he might as well go through with the matter. 'Regarding that crater, Dr. Blair, it is more than probable that below it there exists a section of the Jurassic Age, which has remained untouched for eighty million years.'

'I am aware of that. Mr. Masterson made that point very clear when he contacted me. The pity was that the shaft was sealed before my colleagues and I could investigate.'

'You still can when the volcanic discharge has stopped.'

'*If* it stops. I personally don't think it will. Britain has been provided with a volcano, thanks to you and your men opening up a volcanic seam.'

'Which to my mind may be a blessing in disguise,' Cliff said urgently. 'Doesn't it occur to you, doctor, that if pterodactyls existed down there — as we know they did — there might also be other forms of prehistoric life? Thanks to the volcanic upheaval going on they cannot escape into the outer world and cause havoc amongst us. Indeed they may all have been destroyed. That is one of the points I wanted to mention to you. Despite the loss to science, it would be just as well if that portion of the Jurassic Age has been wiped out.'

'Cold comfort, Mr. Brooks, but I see your point.'

'On the other hand you should study the nature of the gases being discharged from that volcanic region. The main blow-out was caused by pure nitrogene gas, according to our mining chemists.'

'Nitrogene?' The scientist reflected for a moment. 'Let me think now — That's a gas common to volcanic discharge. Well, supposing it is present? It doesn't signify, does it?'

'It might. Our chemists tried pure nitrogene gas on two rabbits, and they were transformed into killers almost immediately. I've had time to think a lot lying here,' Cliff continued. 'It seems to me that if nitrogene gas in the pure state can produce killer instincts in harmless rabbits, then in the adulterated state — mixed with the atmospheric gases, I mean — it might produce a mild toxicosis in the form of sheer bad temper amongst humans. Add to that the sudden increase in crime, the decline in self-respect, and it may add up to something.'

Dr. Blair fingered his lips pensively. 'I see what you mean. But surely there isn't enough nitrogene being emitted to impregnate the atmosphere! Think of the atmosphere's depth.'

'I am doing — and I'm also remembering that the epidemic of bad manners and so forth is local. You don't hear any change much beyond London, though we may later. The degeneration is roughly fixed within an area of twenty miles, with the volcanic region at the centre. I'm sure that isn't coincidence.'

Blair pondered again. It was clear that the theory had caught him by surprise. It was also clear, from his next words, that he could not find any holes in it, either.

'Gases of various types produce varying results on the human frame,' he admitted, 'so perhaps nitrogene is responsible for the strange change in Londoners. What do we do about it then? We can't seal off the gas seepage without causing more volcanic trouble — '

'We can't seal off the gas even if we wanted,' Cliff interrupted. 'The crater is too large for one thing, and at the moment too hot for another. We've got to wait until things cool off somewhat. There's also another side to the business. The presence of nitrogene gas may be the very reason why prehistoric creatures have survived below in the way they have. I don't mean as eggs, but as living creatures. I notice from the reports that the pterodactyls which have been destroyed have been pronounced in the full vigour of health, as perfect as they were eighty million years ago.'

'You're not suggesting that they have lived for that length of time, are you?' Blair's eyes were sharp.

'Why not? The monsters of the past were known to have lives of vast length. Given a particular type of gas that prevents the slow breakdown of cellular tissue, always the cause of death, there's no reason why they should not survive almost eternally. And that raises the question of creatures other than pterodactyls that may be surviving in the depths, only prevented from being loosed upon us by the volcanic fires. Now you realise why I said the volcano trouble is a blessing in disguise.'

Blair seemed to remember something. 'A little while ago you made reference to monsters as living creatures, apart from the egg form. What put the idea of an egg in your mind?'

'Oh, just inference.' Cliff's expression gave nothing away. 'All the monsters of the Jurassic and Mesozoic periods came from eggs — '

'Yes — I see what you mean. Well, in regard to this theory of yours, what do we do about it? We can't stop the gas, yet if we don't people may become even more affected by it, and its density may spread finally to involve the entire atmospheric envelope. On the other hand, if the crater cools off and the gas ceases we may get incredible creatures emerging from below ... We might even have a clash of the Jurassic and Modern periods and that would be fantastic.'

'For the time being,' Cliff answered, 'we can only watch and observe what happens. If there's no improvement I have an idea that may help us — but I want to think about it first. What I want you to do is particularly observe what effect nitrogene gas is having on human beings and animals. You have the instruments and the experience necessary for detailed study, whereas I have not. In any case, I'm not fit to tackle anything much at the moment, so it's up to you and your fellow scientists.'

Blair departed shortly afterwards, and Joan came up into the bedroom, her eyes enquiring.

'Anything interesting?' she asked. 'He seemed rather less like a bear with a sore head after you'd finished with him.'

'Probably because I gave him something to think about. As a matter of fact, Joan, I'm working on an idea that is pretty startling and most certainly dangerous. Yet somehow I can't resist it. If we accept the fact that this gas and volcanic discharge is not going to stop — and that seems to be the possibility — we've got to find a way of *making* it do so. The answer to that one is to go below and seal the fissure from where the trouble is coming and divert it into some other channel, some natural volcanic vent whereby it will be discharged in the proper manner through volcanic means.'

'Well, isn't that what's happening now? If that thing in the basalt area isn't a volcanic crater I don't know what is!'

'Of course it is, but Britain is too small to stand a flashpoint as dangerous as that.

It must be diverted to a volcanic core already in existence, the nearest one being Vesuvius in Italy.'

Joan's eyes widened. 'How on earth do you propose to do that?'

'By going down deeply enough to be able to contact a fire tributary to Vesuvius. When that is done the volcanic trouble in the seat of the basalt centre must be diverted to there by underground engineering. It will be long and difficult, but it has to be done.'

'And the poor Italians will get the benefit!'

'Not at all. Vesuvius is always discharging foul gases, and probably nitrogene, but there are so many other gases as well . . . In England here we've got it in the pure state, and apparently the atmospheric gases can't altogether cancel it out.'

Joan began to look even more troubled. 'I don't understand a thing about underground engineering, Cliff, but even I can see that you'll have to go down to a tremendous depth. About how far do you think?'

'Fifty miles — maybe a hundred.'

There was only one answer to this. Cliff had not yet fully recovered from his concussion.

'I know what you're thinking,' he smiled, interpreting Joan's expression. 'Of the apparent impossibility of the job. But I'm not a mining engineer for nothing, Joan. I propose that the company should make an atomic bore — a mechanical mole, if you will, with a driving screw at the front and an atomic annihilator at the rear to destroy the stuff that is shifted by the drill. More plainly, I mean we should have a machine to enable us to go down a hundred, or even a thousand miles, if need be. At least to the core of this volcanic trouble. The whole problem is one of stresses and strains, since the pressure will increase with every mile we go down. But I think it can be done. Years ago, when I first joined the company, I had the sketch of such a mechanical borer, but I never went any further with it. Now I think is the time to work on it again, particularly since I'm laid up here.'

Once again Joan's main trouble was her

lack of imagination. She could not visualise what Cliff meant. Perhaps this was not surprising, since she had never been any further underground than a tube station. Further, she could not foresee any real danger, either, once again because she lacked imagination. The fact that the nitrogene gas polluting the atmosphere might reach a stage where it impregnated the entire atmospheric envelope with toxicity never occurred to her.

With Cliff, though, the problem was a very real one, and he spent the monotonous hours thinking it over and drawing sketches at intervals with his one useful hand. Day succeeded day, and each day brought news of some depredation or other that could be traced to the activity of nitrogene gas. Crime was still on the upswing, and the general 'couldn't care less' attitude of men and women was on the increase. With children the effect seemed to be different. They tended instead towards destructive notions, ranging from fighting each other to a standstill to breaking windows with stones. And the basalt crater still smoked on.

Meanwhile, nearer home, Herbert was still growing. In the course of a further week he had nearly doubled his size and ate everything that came his way, together with six full buckets of water every day to slake his thirst. Each day, held by the chain about Joan's wrist, he came in to see Cliff, studied him with his red eyes, licked him with his nutmeg grater tongue and was then taken out again to his garage kennel. Both Joan and Cliff knew they were harbouring an abnormality, but just the same their affection for the ugly brute outweighed the thought of consequences.

Then, about a fortnight after his first visit, Dr. Blair returned, his manner still sharp and on the edge of rudeness. To this Cliff paid little attention, quite convinced in his own mind that it was not the scientist's own fault.

'I've made all the necessary tests on nitrogene, Mr. Brooks,' he announced, 'and there's no doubt of the fact that it *is* the cause of the present atavism amongst men and women. It is causing a complete and dangerous degeneration — though you probably know all about that from the news reports.

'Yes, I know,' Cliff assented grimly.

'We had volunteers upon whom we experimented, both men and women, and when they were subjected to pure nitrogene gas drawn off from the volcanic site itself they exhibited all the signs of primitive people. In a way their features seemed to change, too. They became blunter, almost Neanderthal. In my opinion,' Blair finished, 'the trouble is spreading rapidly, out from the centre which is the basalt crater. Formerly it was just London that seemed to be involved. Now it is most of the country. I'm expecting any minute to hear of this atavism affecting our nearest foreign neighbours.'

'Which means the impregnation of the atmosphere with this nitrogene gas is becoming more intensive.'

'Exactly. Just as you assumed it would.' Blair tapped his fingers on his bony knees and tightened his lips. 'We just don't know what to do about it. It's causing chaos in all directions. We're not progressing; we're sliding down the evolutionary scale. If this goes on we'll finish up as troglodytes, no longer interested in or able to control the mighty cities and sciences we've built up through endless generations.'

'And the crater?' Cliff asked. 'How is that going on?'

'It's now cool enough to enter for exploration purposes. I did so a few days ago with a party of chosen scientists, all of us wearing respirators, which prevented the nitrogene affecting us. We traced the gas leak with our instruments — if one can call it a leak when the stuff is pouring out of a bottomless shaft nearly two miles in width! To seal that up, even if we dared, is impossible.'

'And you found the gas filling the entire two mile area?'

'We did, yes. Here are some photographs that will interest you. You'll see that the shaft is not sheer. It curves as it descends.'

Cliff took the prints and examined them carefully. They depicted vast areas of blackened rock where cooling had taken place, together with solidified slag and lava.

'Bad,' Cliff muttered. 'Very bad. Since the shaft is on the slant it means that any animals that may be below can find a way up. They couldn't have done it up a sheer wall, but they can up this.'

'My worry, too,' Blair said. 'Up to now the heat has kept any animals away, granting they survived, but now things have cooled off anything can happen. I hesitate to tell the authorities to give a general alarm for fear the panic is worse than the possible arrival of prehistoric animals. Altogether it is a very nasty position. You said last time I was here that you might have an answer to it all. Do you still say that?'

'I do, and even more vehemently. In the past two weeks I have worked out the design of an earth-bore, a kind of land submarine for driving into the lower depths. My original idea was to use it for finding a way to divert the volcanic discharge to more natural outlets, but since that seems to have died out I needn't to worry over it, thank heaven. But I still think the source of this nitrogene gas must be found and, if possible, obliterated.'

Cliff picked up a folder from his bedside table and opened it. 'It will be a week at least before I'll be allowed to start moving around,' he explained. 'And probably a week after that before I can interest my company in this idea. This being so, I'm delegating you to do it. Time's precious, and if they approve the idea they can start to build the earth-bore right away.'

Blair nodded, examining the sketches and specifications with a professional eye.

'The principle of it is quite within bounds,' Cliff explained. 'We have the machine itself, built exactly on the lines of a submarine, only of specially toughened tungsten steel capable of withstanding colossal pressures and strains without buckling. Similar stuff is used these days for deep-sea diving bells so there'll be no difficulty. To lessen the strain of rock pressure there's this atomic field entirely round the vessel, which acts as a partial repulsor to inwardly pressing strains. A total repulsor is too advanced an idea to be perfected as yet, by me, anyway. At the front we have the claw that

80

holds the drill, the drills being of different gauges according to the work to be done. Motive power is from a two million horse power atomic engine which ought to be powerful enough to force through anything. Finally there is this improvement on the endless belt system whereby the material chewed away by the drill is carried through these channels to the rear of the machine and destroyed atomically by the exhausts. That way we dispose of the problem of excavated material.'

'And the inside of the vessel on gyroscopic bearings so it always stays upright,' Blair mused. 'Yes, an excellent idea. I should imagine it would be possible to penetrate to a considerable depth with this.'

'A thousand miles and more, maybe,' Cliff reflected. 'My idea is twofold, Dr. Blair. For one thing I want to get this nitrogene gas trouble stopped at the source, and if there is a Jurassic region area left below I want to have a look at it. Also I'm still anxious to discover what lies at the bottom of the giant inner canyon I discovered. Curiosity drives one to do odd things sometimes, and the earth-bore is my way of trying to satisfy that curiosity.'

Blair got to his feet and folded the sketches carefully. 'I'll see what I can do, Mr. Brooks — on one condition.'

'Is this a time to make conditions with general atavism threatening?'

'It's nothing very terrible I want — merely to come with you when you delve below. Possibly some of my fellow scientists as well if there's room. Don't forget we were going to look at the Jurassic region on Masterson's invitation. In the earth-bore we can perhaps still do it.'

Cliff held out his free hand. 'Done! Let me know how you get on.'

4

Dinosaur attack

Dr. Blair wasted no time in dealing with the mining company, and he probably made a much more convincing job of things than Cliff could ever have done, because he was a scientist with a much-respected name. The mining company finally consented to finance the project, not so much because they believed nitrogene gas was causing atavism, nor because they were afraid of the advent of prehistoric monsters. Their one stake in the whole thing was that they could obtain samples of the underworld by this means, which could never be done any other way. The earth-bore opened up the prospect of the mining company becoming the most efficient underground specialists in the world.

So the earth-bore was put in hand with the promise of a considerable financial return to Cliff later if the machine lived up to all he claimed for it. The decision put him on his feet faster than anything, and he waited anxiously for news of the vessel's completion. In the meantime the reports of the nitrogene gas's ravages were anything but encouraging. It was definitely producing a slowing up of all usual activities. Business was indifferently attended to, or else not at all, so extreme was the apathy in these late summer days. Many streets were left uncleaned, with the inevitable consequence of epidemics. Everything seemed to be too much trouble, from the highest to the lowest in the land. There was more and more tendency to take whatever one needed without consulting the owner thereof — usually through the medium of violence or actual murder.

To Cliff, watching the situation, it was perfectly clear what was happening. Every man, woman and child in England — and in parts of Europe and America, too, now — was breathing in the toxic fumes which completely upset the nervous system and tended to slow up the action of the brain.

Eighty million years earlier this gas had existed in the atmosphere of the Jurassic and Mesozoic Ages in considerable preponderance — and now it was assuming the same preponderance again. By this process it was reducing mankind back to the state he had reached in earlier times — which, if it did nothing else, proved the theory that Man is only what he is because of the atmosphere he breathes. If the outflow of nitrogene from its apparently inexhaustible source within the earth were not stopped, there was nothing to stop Man returning to the caveman era, along with the beasts that had existed in and around that same epoch.

As yet nobody knew the cause of the drift into idleness, crime, and the baser instincts. Nobody knew why high intellects had toppled and why brute force appealed far more than mental adroitness. Cliff had not said a word and neither had the scientists. Where was the sense of doing so? If the gas were stopped that would end the trouble, and the atmosphere would gradually sweeten out again. It would be time enough to speak if the trouble could not be overcome. And even then the obvious solution of providing tens of millions of respirators for every man, woman and child in the world — if the nitrogene spread that far — was not practicable. Human beings could not spend the rest of their lives in masks, snatching at meals as best they could. No, all things considered, Cliff was satisfied that he had made the only possible move.

But an incident one evening showed that the gas was not the only thing that had to be conquered. Cliff's second theory that monsters might escape from the buried Jurassic region came true. The first warning came from two young lovers sitting in the summer dusk of a country lane not very far from the basalt site. The stars had only just come into view, and there hung over everything the quiet calm of the twilight. They murmured to each other as lovers will, promising each other practically every impossible thing, all natural romance blasted out of their sentiments by the insidious nitrogene and its place taken by nothing more than plain lust.

Then the head appeared over the nearby rise in the meadow. The young man saw it first. He had the girl in his arms at the time, and when he saw the head he mistook it for a rock — until it moved. It became larger against the stars, larger still, and still larger.

'Wha — wha — what is it?' the girl stammered hoarsely, seeing it and feeling the young man trembling as he held her.

'Martians,' he panted, his mind flavoured by the entertainment of the times. 'Or — or something! Glory be — ' A head the size of a bus, a neck the length of a railway carriage, and then the body. As big as a house, two houses, three houses! And a tail that lashed slowly back and forth, setting up eddies in the still air. There it towered at the top of the bank, its mighty front legs thicker than telegraph poles, abysmal rumbles coming from the head, where the cavernous mouth lay.

'Run for it!' the young man yelled, whirling the girl around. 'It's a monster of some sort — Run for your life!'

He forgot all about romance and the male instinct to protect his intended mate. He took to his heels and flew down the lane at a speed that would have made a track runner's eyes goggle. The girl looked after him in sickened bewilderment, paralysed, a tiny figure in front of the colossus as it began to move down the bank.

The fact that she remained still saved the girl's life. She was so tiny the mighty dinosaur did not even see her in the twilight. His vast body went right over her as she fell screaming in the dust, covered for a moment by the massive grey belly with the pillars of legs. She tried to get up at the last moment, but a twitch of the advancing monster's tail, struck her across the shoulder. Bones splintered and she was flung half a dozen yards over the hedge and into the field beyond. She was still alive yes, but with her arm and shoulder smashed to pulp with that playful tap.

The monster was still not aware of her. Its attention was riveted on that hurtling speck flying down the lane. With a noise like an express train, the ground shaking with the concussion of the enormous feet, the dinosaur bore down on the hapless young man in eighty odd tons of fury. He never knew what hit him. A foot came down, and that was that. The vast mouth opened, tossed the corpse around and then spat it out. Head reared, little red eyes aflame, the creature from eighty million years ago sniffed the nitrogene in the breeze, liked it, and looked around for further prey.

Lumbering, it went up the bank again, pushing a stone pylon out of its way and bringing down a twisted mass of broken high-tension wires. They flashed and sparkled on its grey armour-clad back, but no twitch of death affected that immensely powerful heart. True, the brute jolted for a moment, then it tore free of 30,000 volts and resumed its juggernaut progress.

That was how things began. Towards midnight the injured girl who had literally had a brush with the monster crawled into the village police station, gave a gasping account of her adventure and then collapsed. Police everywhere were alerted, as they had been at the time of the pterodactyls, and the various home defence units of the Army were ordered out to seek the dinosaur.

They found it — or at least they thought they did. What they did not know was that it was another one, the original colossus still being on the prowl somewhere in the countryside.

Through the night the danger grew. By three in the morning half a dozen monsters had been sighted, not all of them identical in appearance, either. Some had spiked backs, others had extra long necks, some were less fearsome than others in size, but every one of them was of the Jurassic Age and deadly dangerous to encounter. Out went the radio and television warnings, but at that hour of night most people were asleep and knew nothing of what was going on.

Cliff and Joan were no exceptions. They were blissfully asleep as one of the dinosaurs — the original one as a matter of fact — came across the fields to the rear of their home moving like a gargantuan elephant in the pale summer moonlight. It stopped now and again to scent the breeze, and it was not altogether the nitrogene it liked, either. There was something else, something that finally directed its slow-moving body in the direction of the Brooks' garage.

The high fence round the garden crumpled up like matchsticks as the dinosaur trampled it out of the way. Its eighty tons of weight flattened out the flowerbeds and left dents in the lawn. Then it reached the garage, towering over its roofs, its mighty head inclined towards the doors and its snout twitching gently.

Suddenly, from within the garage, there was a frightful scream. It was neither human nor animal: it was something out of the misty reaches of Jurassic times, more blood-curdling than the wail of a coyote or the insane laughter of the hyena. It was Herbert, making the first noise of his young life, a noise begotten of sheer excitement at the realisation that one of his own kind was close at hand.

The scream awoke Joan, though she

did not immediately grasp what was wrong. She lay wondering, then when the scream came again she really awakened with a vengeance. Startled, she scrambled out of bed and tumbled sleepily to the window. But the window was blotted out by a mountain of grey reaching well above the top of the house.

'Cliff!' she yelled desperately. 'Cliff, for heaven's sake — '

Cliff jolted out of slumber and opened his eyes. 'What?' he mumbled. 'What's wrong? What are y'doing there?'

'There's a monster or something trying to get at Herbert! Come and look!'

Still half-asleep, and not able to move with any freedom even yet, Cliff struggled out of bed, fully convinced that Joan had been having a nightmare. He instantly revised his opinion when he saw the 'backside' of the dinosaur against the window, one of its huge forefeet kicking experimentally at the garage doors.

'For the love of Pete!' Cliff gasped hoarsely. 'Look at the size of that thing — ! Do you know what it is?'

'No — and I don't care. Cliff, what do

we do? If it backs into the house the walls will just fall apart.'

'Looks like a diplodocus to me,' Cliff muttered. 'Look at the frilly effect round his neck — No, I don't think he's a diplodocus. Perhaps a tyrannosaurus — '

'Who cares?' Joan shouted hysterically. 'Let's get out of here into the open. Can you manage that?'

'Yes — I suppose so. If there's real need, that is. He's far more interested in Herbert than in us at the moment.'

'You — you think that's what he's looking for?'

'Obvious, isn't it?'

It certainly was — horrifyingly so. Joan remembered how the pterodactyl had made the same effort to get at the then unhatched Herbert: now the same thing was happening again.

'Must be some sort of instinct these brutes have,' Cliff murmured, obviously far more fascinated than horrified. 'But I don't like the idea of Herbert falling foul of this brute.'

'Neither do I,' Joan snapped. 'I've brought Herbert up from — from an egg, and I'm more than devoted to him. I'm going to do something about it,' she finished decisively, and Cliff gave her a wondering glance in the moonlight.

'Nothing you can do,' he said. 'Unless, of course, you're asking to be killed.'

For answer Joan swung round, pulled on her gown and slippers, and then left the room. Cliff muttered to himself and hobbled to the door, snatching it open.

'Joan! Come back here! Don't do anything silly!'

He imagined she had gone downstairs to attempt some foolhardy stunt with the monster out in the open — but in a moment she appeared from the bathroom gingerly carrying something in a glass jar. Cliff watched her as she came up.

'What on earth's that?' he demanded. 'Water? You don't suppose water will — '

'Sulphuric acid,' she interrupted tautly. 'Had you forgotten you've a bottle of the beastly stuff in the bathroom there for when you do your cine-photography? If this doesn't make the brute jump nothing will!'

'Joan, don't be an idiot!' Cliff would

have grabbed her if the risk of spilling the acid had not been so great. 'The brute will probably kick like all hell when that stuff gets on it, and if it does the house will go over.'

'He's not taking little Herbert!' Joan insisted, and with that she strode resolutely across the bedroom, set down the sulphuric acid on the ledge and opened the window gently. At that same moment the dinosaur, tired of snuffling and unable to get into the garage, slammed up his 'knee' and sent it crashing straight through the garage doors. They swung drunkenly on their hinges. The mighty body heaved forward, and wood cracked and splintered under the advance. From the debris beyond came the pitiful howling of Herbert. And by this time there wasn't a neighbour in the whole district who was not awake and wondering what the blue blazes was happening.

'You filthy, great brute!' Joan shouted furiously, a curiously deflected mother love urging her to protect Herbert with everything she'd got. 'I'll show you!'

She flung the acid cleanly and neatly, knowing from experience its syrupy, clinging quality. The stuff splashed on the armoured hide and sizzled horribly. For a second or two there was no effect — then with a snarling, ground-shaking rumble the dinosaur reared up and swung around in its own length, seeking the cause of the pain eating into its tough skin. Probably it was having no more serious effect than a cigarette stub burning human flesh, but it was enough to annoy the colossus more than somewhat.

Joan dodged back as the mighty head swung and the hardly visible eyes studied the house. It evidently dawned on the tiny brain that the cause of the trouble lay there, for the brute suddenly charged with malignant fury, its head down. The wall of the house buckled inwards under the terrific impact. Floors and ceiling swayed. With a scream Joan felt herself flying through dusty chips and nothingness, to at last land flat on her back with all the breath knocked out of her. Covering her head with her hands she listened to earth-shaking roars of fury and felt the reverberation of massive feet amid the further collapse of walls.

Then things began to quiet down and she stirred slowly, looking about her in the moonlight. It gradually became clear to her that part, but not all, of the floor above had fallen through, and she had gone with the collapse. Some of the wall had come down, too. The other half of the floor still remained, and upon it Cliff was evidently quite safe, for his voice floated down.

'You okay, Joan?'

'More or less. How about you?'

'Not so bad. I caught hold of the doorway when the floor went, and it saved me. Good job, too. I can't afford more broken bones with these others only just knit together. If I can find a staircase I'll come down.'

Sounds above and a shifting and scrambling in the shattered house. Then the voices of neighbours. Joan got to her feet, drew the girdle of her dusty dressing gown about her, and looked through the great hole in the wall towards the garage. There was a good deal of plaintive howling from Herbert, but the dinosaur had gone! Joan smiled triumphantly to herself. Evidently it did not like sulphuric acid.

Then the next door neighbour came into the garden over the smashed fence, his voice high with questions. By the time Cliff had found his way downstairs there were quite a number of men and women present in the shattered lounge, all of them in night attire, some frightened and others downright angry.

'Look here, Mr. Brooks,' said the neighbour from the opposite side, 'this is the second time there's been some kind of trouble here. First it was a pterodactyl; this time it was an elephant, or something.'

'It was a dinosaur,' Cliff said coldly. 'And you don't suppose I invited it here, do you?'

'Dinosaur? Did you say dinosaur? But there haven't been things like that for — for donkey's years. Mmmm, there was the pterodactyl, of course.'

'That creature — the dinosaur I mean — came from the basalt crater,' Cliff continued, making no effort to conceal anything. 'Probably there will be others.'

'Then why the devil should these things always make for this part? There's something here they seem to like, and whatever it is it wants exposing.'

Cliff was silent, but unfortunately for him Herbert gave a frightful howl at that very moment. The irate neighbour, his own house cracked to demolition point, looked sharply towards the hole in the wall.

'What's that?' he snapped.

'Certainly wasn't cats,' his wife said, her arms folded under her pendulous bust.

'Don't be an idiot, Daisy!' And the irate neighbour plunged through the hole in the wall and strode over to the wrecked garage, staring at it in the moonlight. It was wrecked, yes, but the woodwork was jammed so completely in all directions that nothing could escape from within.

'Come away from there!' Joan shouted in fury. 'Mr. Bentley! You hear me? That is not your property!'

'If it's concerned with my property

being wrecked, Mrs. Brooks, it's only logical for me to look.'

Bentley grabbed the shattered doors and pulled furiously. They parted easily enough and he stumbled backwards and sat down with a painful bump. When he started to get up again he paused, staring blankly at Herbert's unlovely face in the moonlight

Plainly, Herbert was annoyed as well as frightened. He did not recognise Bentley's face and he did not like him either. So he advanced, rumbling in his thick throat, upper lip drawn back over triple rows of teeth.

'Help, for God's sake!' Bentley screamed. 'It's something out of — '

'Herbert!' Joan commanded imperiously. 'Herbert, come here!'

The infant monster hesitated, chewing his growling and breathing foetidly — but he obeyed. Slowly he lumbered forward and stopped at Joan's side. The neighbours backed away, and for this they could hardly be blamed. Herbert was as big as a Shetland pony and about ten thousand times fiercer.

'Better go whilst you're safe, Mr. Bentley,' Cliff said brusquely. 'Now you know what's in the garage and the probable reason for prehistoric monsters trying to get at it. It is a prehistoric monster itself, so probably there's an affinity.'

Bentley got up, smouldering with fury. 'Look, Mr. Brooks, if you think you can get away with this you're vastly mistaken! That thing isn't only a menace in itself; it's a menace in that it attracts other — '

Bentley's remaining words were drowned out. From the garden there suddenly came the ground-shaking roar of a full-grown dinosaur followed by the thunder of advancing feet. Before anybody fully realised what had happened, the dinosaur of the earlier visit returned to the scene, smashing down the sagging wall in its onrush.

'Out!' Cliff yelled. 'Out, everybody!'

His warning was necessary as far as dodging the slowly falling house was concerned, but not in regard to the monster. It did not even seem to notice the humans scurrying out of the collapsing lounge and through the hall, never even saw Cliff limping gamely in the rear. Its sole interest was the now deserted Herbert.

Down came the cavernous jaws, closing about Herbert's plump body. He was lifted with an astonishing gentleness, as a cat will lift her kittens. And, satisfied, the dinosaur withdrew from the wreckage, lumbered over the garden and went up the rise of the field towards the night.

Cliff, Joan and the neighbours outside the wrecked house in the street saw the dinosaur departing, something in its jaws but Joan was the first to realise the truth.

'He's taken Herbert! Cliff, he's taken Herbert!'

'Nothing I can do,' Cliff said. 'Just the same I'm as sorry as you are.'

'Sorry!' Bentley choked. 'Dammit, Brooks, you don't seem to realise that in harbouring that little beast you have caused a vast amount of damage — I'm going to inform the police about this.'

'Go ahead,' Cliff sighed. 'I imagine the police have enough to do tonight without listening to your complaint.'

Such indeed was the case, and in any

case Bentley could not telephone because with the collapse of the house, and his own house, too, all wires had been torn away. Herbert apart, however, the militia and police were busy answering calls all night. By dawn, two dinosaurs had been slain and another four were being carefully tracked down. The only thing that killed them were armour-piercing shells. Ordinary gunfire had not the slightest effect.

By dawn also, Cliff's and Bentley's homes were not the only ones in ruins. Dozens of houses had been smashed by careless perambulations of the monsters, power lines were in chaos, telephone wires were broken, smaller bridges had collapsed. The authorities were fuming and so was the populace. Most men and women had sunk into a state of agreeable apathy where nothing seemed to matter — and now this terror had been sprung upon them.

Cliff and Joan had only one move they could make. They salved their most needed possessions from the wreckage and then put up at the local hotel. It was here that Dr. Blair found them the following morning, morose and grim.

'Things are happening with a vengeance,' he said as he joined Cliff and Joan in the lounge.

'We're already aware of that,' Cliff growled, and he gave a detailed account of what had happened in the night, none the less deliberately omitting Herbert.

'Your case is by no means isolated,' Blair responded. 'Even the media haven't covered all the details. I have, because my fellow scientists and I have asked for direct information on everything that happens. You'll be interested to know that nearly thirty prehistoric creatures of every type and description found their way out of the basalt crater during the night! They were counted by the special scientific watchmen we have there. Radio information was sent to us immediately. There were recognisable specimens of the triceratops, diplodocus, iguanodon, pterodactyl, tyrannosaurus and several others. Out of that number two — two! — have been destroyed. The others are rambling around wreaking death and destruction.

Except the iguanodon, which is mainly herbivorous and isn't interested in animals and humans. Do you realize what it means?'

'Naturally,' Cliff answered. 'In the present state of human lethargy it means that most of our civilisation is going to be smashed down by these Jurassic brutes unless the militia can work fast enough to kill them off — '

'I can't see that happening,' Blair interrupted. 'Just before coming here I received news that further monsters are still emerging from the crater. The Army is going to move up there and slay them as they come out, but if there are great numbers of them that battle may go on for years. There is also another peculiar point. Every animal which has appeared is female.'

Cliff gave a start. 'Are your watchers sure of that?'

'Certainly. They had searchlights on every animal in the hope of turning it back. That hope was not realized — but the glare showed up the anatomical formation. Every one female. I just don't understand it.'

Cliff gave Joan a significant glance. Herbert had been male: no doubt of that.

'I mean,' Blair continued, 'how could the race of monsters have propagated as it has if there are only females? There must be males somewhere.'

'There is another possibility,' Cliff said slowly. 'It has always been assumed that the monsters of the past died out — apart from some catastrophic event — because they were superseded by smaller, more refined animals. But that is only a theory. There exists now the equally possible theory that the race vanished because the males mysteriously became extinct. Maybe these female animals, left behind from Jurassic times, are just a surviving remnant of the species, kept alive by nitrogene gas, the predominant element in the atmosphere of their time.'

'Maybe,' Blair admitted. 'In any case, Mr. Brooks, it is no longer a matter of theorising. We have got to have action. That earth-bore of yours will be ready the day after tomorrow, I understand, and if you are fit by then to make the journey then let us do so. The monsters and the nitrogene gas have both to be stopped before absolute chaos overwhelms us.'

'We'll go when the bore's ready whether I'm a hundred percent fit or not.' Cliff promised. 'Keep me in touch, Dr.Blair and I'll do the rest.'

'Right.' Blair got to his feet. 'That brings things up to date, and the sooner we get some action the better.'

He shook hands and went on his way, leaving Cliff musing deeply, until Joan interrupted his meditations.

'I suppose it's only coincidence about the escaped animals all being female?'

'I don't think so, Joan. The theory I outlined still stands.'

'But Herbert was male! That shows there are males!'

'Not necessarily. Poor old Herbert was inside an egg, frozen into a glacier, until I found him. We hatched him out all right, but it is possible that the egg would never have hatched but for our intervention. There have been cases even amongst common-or-garden fowls where only the eggs containing hens have hatched and those containing roosters have not. It has something to do with atmospheric and chemical conditions, which is one reason why forced incubation is used so much. That, scientifically, prevents a misfire. The same thing could have happened in the Jurassic Age. Some climatic change, some great elemental disturbance, caused the complete sterility of all male eggs. For that reason the race of monsters died out, except for the surviving few females caught in this one queer area we've discovered.' Cliff hunched forward, brooding. 'Consider the situation now, Joan, and the mess we've made of things! We hatched out Herbert, a male! That accounts, I think, for the instinctive searching by both the pterodactyl and the dinosaur to find him. We can't explain what queer instincts animals possess, but we do know that an attempt has been made to get at Herbert each time.'

'And succeeded!' Joan's face was blank.

'Yes, I'm afraid so. We've provided the prehistoric survivors with a means of perpetuating themselves. Herbert will soon be mature, and when he is he'll obviously mate with a female! Once that happens the prehistoric race can continue to breed! If males also appear amongst the young ones the problem becomes even more complex.'

'And if we hadn't meddled the Jurassic monsters would automatically have died out?'

'Eventually. Knowing their tremendous life span there would not perhaps have been much advantage. The trouble now is that, with Herbert abroad, we can never know when we've come to the end of killing these brutes. More can keep on appearing.'

'Not if we go below and wipe them out or seal them up, or something. That is what we're going to do, isn't it?'

'I am, yes,' Cliff agreed, looking at Joan in surprise. 'You surely don't think you are included, do you?'

'There'll be an awful row if I'm not! I want to find Herbert again if I can. I'll go to any length to do that. A baby dinosaur he may be, but I love him — and in his clumsy way I think he loves us. Me, anyway.'

'Could be,' Cliff conceded, his brow

wrinkled. 'Matter of fact, Joan, you're a considerable surprise to me. The way you threw sulphuric acid at that monster, for one thing. I don't know where you got the nerve!'

'Something came over me,' Joan answered. 'I wasn't a bit afraid. It wasn't altogether because I wanted to save Herbert, either: it was something else. A feeling that I'm a human being with a higher intelligence than that great monster, so it was up to me to send it packing.'

Cliff reflected. 'Probably an answer to that, too. Nitrogene gas.'

'What in the world do you mean?'

'I mean that the fierce primordial courage of the early human beings, like the cave dwellers, was probably caused by the nitrogene gas they were breathing in the atmosphere. They came after the age of monsters, of course, so had none of them to encounter, but they certainly dealt courageously with sabre-toothed tigers, mastodons, mammoths, and heaven knows what. Probably the nitrogene effect on you is to make you more courageous and fierce than lethargic and bad-tempered.'

'Nitrogene or otherwise, I want to go on this trip and I want to find Herbert again.'

'Going on the trip is most unlikely to produce Herbert. We have no reason for supposing he'll go underground, or be taken there by the monster that has abducted him. The most likely possibility is that he'll be shot down with the rest of the dinosaurs roaming the country.'

'That mustn't happen!' Joan muttered. 'Not to Herbert!'

'We can't stop it,' Cliff insisted. 'We daren't even admit he belongs to us the way things are, otherwise we'll get in a frightful mess. He'll have to take his chance.'

'We couldn't somehow let the authorities know not to shoot down a baby dinosaur?'

'No, we could not. He won't be a baby long, anyhow, and we're not sticking our necks out. From the viewpoint of common sense he's better off dead, and quickly, before he can be instrumental in perpetuating his race.'

5

Into the depths

Though he obviously had misgivings, the doctor discharged Cliff later that day as fit enough to resume normal activity, provided he took sensible precautions. Cliff, for his part, did not give his physical condition a second thought: there was important work to be done. He and Joan made the hotel their 'base of operations' and spent most of their time in travelling back and forth to the mining headquarters to study the all but completed earth-bore. The events happening up and down the country were now of secondary interest to them. The news that monsters were being destroyed here and there did not mean a thing, because more would probably arrive to take their place — and in any case the matter of the gradually spreading nitrogene gas had to be dealt with. The one thing to concentrate upon now was the journey below.

Cliff spent most of the evening, after an afternoon's preliminary study of the machine, making sure that all the controls were exactly as he had planned them. Apparently they were. In appearance the machine itself resembled a submarine, except that it had no conning tower or periscope and was fitted with the powerful drill on the nose. To the rear were the atomic exhaust jets and disintegrator chambers. Inside the machine was the control room, observation room and sleeping quarters, together with smaller compartments for stores, spares, and so forth.

Joan took upon herself to handle the matter of provisions, receiving carte blanche from the chairman of the mining organisation to do so. The chairman did not stint on a single thing: he knew Cliff Brooks was an engineer of vision, and he also knew that if this underground project succeeded there was a mint in it for the mining concern as a whole.

Towards midnight Cliff and Joan returned to the hotel, having made their final arrangements with Dr. Blair for him to be present at the mining headquarters at ten the following morning, along with those scientists he wished to bring with him. Cliff had limited the number to two besides Blair. There would be overcrowding otherwise.

The night was peaceful enough — as far as Cliff and Joan were concerned — but the bulletins at breakfast time carried news of further havoc wrought by wandering monsters. Only two more had been killed, whereas at least eighteen had been seen leaving the underworld. Efforts had been made to destroy them as they emerged from their lair, but one of the earliest arrivals, only wounded, had charged in maddened fury upon the gun battery and smashed the equipment to scrap iron, pounding every soldier into pulp before there had been a chance to escape. This had definitely slowed things up a bit.

'What happens,' Joan asked when breakfast was nearly over, 'if the monsters attack our bore as we descend? Had you thought of that? We haven't any weapons on the vessel — not big ones, anyhow, and those flame-jet guns won't be any use against dinosaurs.'

'We're going to risk that chance,' Cliff replied. 'The worst that can happen is for the bore to be lifted in the jaws of one of the bigger creatures. Certainly the machine cannot be crushed, because it is made to withstand the terrific pressures of the underground. We'll get by somehow, and once we have located the source of the nitrogene gas and blocked it up for good, half the battle will be over. Candidly, I should not be at all surprised if the monsters don't die when nitrogene is cut off. I'm convinced it is only that which keeps them going and which has preserved them through the vast spans of time since the Jurassic epoch. Haven't you noticed in the news reports that they have only been seen in areas where the nitrogene is present in the atmosphere? Beyond its limits there is no trace of them. That speaks for itself.'

Joan nodded and said no more. Now the hour of departure was so near she could not help thinking of all the unpleasant possibilities, but this in no wise changed her determination to make the trip. In any case she'd never have an easy moment without Cliff, even less so with monsters on the prowl and human behaviour at its lowest ebb.

'Time to be going,' Cliff said finally, glancing at his watch. 'I've made all the necessary arrangements with the manager here. He'll keep our room until we return — and of course he doesn't know where we're headed for or he'd be a very surprised man. Better get our things and be off.'

In half an hour the hotel taxi had brought them to the mining headquarters and they made their way to the open field in front of the big workshop where the bore had been made. In a moment or two they came within sight of the machine itself. It had been brought out of its 'home' in readiness to start its journey. Around it, waiting, were Dr. Blair, his two scientific colleagues, the chairman of the mining company, and — inevitably — one or two reporters.

The reporters were soon dealt with. The bore was to be used for testing deep mining. To state its real purpose would not be a good policy unless something had been accomplished. Then, the reporters out of the way, Cliff turned to Dr. Blair and the scientists. They were introduced as Martin Dagman, the famous geologist, a square-faced, stocky man with humorous eyes; and Colin Naysmith, a specialist on prehistoric animals and their habits. He was tall as Dagman was short — a sandy-haired, gangling giant of a man whom it was impossible to dislike.

'Which completes the merry party,' Blair said, rubbing his hands. 'I take it, Mr. Brooks, that everything is set fair for the trip?'

'Everything. My wife here has dealt with the provision and clothing problems — the main items. Correct, Joan?'

'Correct,' she assented. 'Including the new type helmet masks for the nitrogene. If we get to it at close quarters we'll need full protection. And there are enough clothes for all of us for all temperatures from arctic to tropical.'

'What exactly is your plan of attack?'

Naysmith questioned. 'Blair here doesn't seem to know.'

'We start from the basalt crater itself,' Cliff replied, 'following the track downwards into the depths. We'll go overland to get there using the tractors. Now, shall we get started?'

He motioned to the bore, and one by one the menfolk followed Joan into the control room. The chairman of the mining company shook Cliff's hand warmly.

'Our good wishes go with you, Cliff,' he smiled. 'You can say you're doing this to chase monsters and stop poison gas, but to me it's still a project for future mining — and there's a fortune in it for you if it works. So, good luck!'

'Thanks, sir,' Cliff smiled. 'We'll do our best.'

He closed the airlock tightly and bolted it, then crossed to the control board. Around him the others settled down in the softly-sprung seats and kept their eyes on the big reflecting mirror which gave a perfect prismatic view of exterior conditions.

'Ready?' Cliff questioned, and heads nodded promptly.

He switched on the power to half, more than sufficient for ordinary land movement Another lever released caterpillar wheels under the base of the machine and it began to move forward across the field. There was nothing particularly thrilling about this: it had no more interest value than travelling in a tank, except that no tank had ever been so well sprung, the interior cabin being completely separated by its air-cushioned bearings from the immensely tough outer shell.

Cruising at a comfortable thirty miles an hour the bore sped across the field, through a hedge and so reached the main road. Then it proceeded on its way like any other vehicle, the only difference being that its strangeness of design caused passers-by to gaze in amazement, whilst here and there were nearly traffic incidents as car and lorry drivers forgot their own jobs in gazing at the weird land-submarine.

It took Cliff twenty minutes to reach the basalt site. Here the Army units were gathered, together with two sentries at the main entrance. Cliff lowered the steel-plated shutter at his side.

'Carry on, sir,' the sentry said, peering in curiously.

'How are things going?' Blair asked anxiously.

'We've got a fresh gun unit into position, doctor, after the mess up with the last one. Haven't been any more monsters for the last five hours. And though it's not my place to say so, I wouldn't give much for your chances if you meet up with one of them.'

'That's our worry,' Cliff smiled. 'Thanks, sentry.'

He closed the slide and drove forward, the outer shell heaving and rocking as the tractor teeth clawed over the uneven rocks until finally the edge of the crater was reached. It was not smoking any more: it just yawned there, the gate to the abyss.

Cliff stopped the machine and looked at the quiet, tense faces.

'This is it,' he said. 'We may never come up again. If any of you here wishes to get out, then do so. You'll not be thought the worse of.'

Nobody moved.

'Right,' Cliff said. 'Here we go.'

He put the machine in gear again and it began to lumber down the rocky slope leading to the heart of the crater. All eyes turned to the prismatic mirror that reflected the rocky walls gliding past. Then after a moment or two the brilliant morning sunlight vanished. Immediately Cliff switched on the searchlights, which resulted in a view of the downward sloping declivity they were pursuing. At the moment everything was just routine. They were merely pursuing the ordinary journey down the crater's side, a trip that Cliff had already made before the big blowout.

'No signs of monsters,' the geologist commented.

'Just as well,' Blair responded. 'I for one am not dying to meet a dinosaur.'

The crater ended at 300 feet depth, opening out into what had formerly been the area that Cliff had explored — the cavern of stalactites and glacier wall. Now the stalactites and glacier wall had gone, and instead there was solidified plasma and pumice rock.

'The eruption didn't come from here anyway,' the geologist decided, watching intently as the screen mirrored everything. 'Must have come from lower down — '

'Yes,' Cliff muttered. 'From that bottomless canyon, I'll wager. At least I call it bottomless to give an idea of its depth. Over here somewhere — '

He swung the nose of the bore to the right and reduced speed to a minimum. At length he came to the very edge of the underground chasm. Cliff cut off the power and turned.

'Might do worse than get out and see what's ahead of us — or rather below.'

The others rose immediately and Blair opened the airlock.

The air that came surging in was warm and unpleasant to inhale.

Plainly there was a good deal of sulphur and volcanic gas mixed in it — and probably plenty of nitrogene, too, only it could not make itself evident amongst such a heavy preponderance of other elements.

'Better use the masks,' Cliff advised. 'We don't want to be choked before we even start!'

Joan turned and headed for the store cupboard, returning presently with five masks rather after the style of goldfish bowls.

They were a distinct improvement on the ordinary kind of respirator, far less suffocating in use and enabling the wearer to have complete vision in all directions. Further, each one was equipped with radio pick-ups fitted into the collar and supplied with dry batteries. Thereby, any words were amplified outside the mask, and the resonance thereof was quite sufficient to penetrate the helmet without need of earphones.

Once they had their helmets in place and the subsidiary oxygen cylinders strapped to their backs, Cliff led the way outside and then stood on the edge of the chasm surveying the scene below. It looked very much to him as it had on the previous occasion. The same conviction of infinite depth, and the queer phosphorescent quality. The only difference lay in the side of the chasm. Formerly, before the volcanic outburst, it had been almost sheer. Now it sloped noticeably.

'Do you think it's possible to get the bore down this chasm side?' asked Colin Naysmith, the lank expert on prehistory.

'No,' Cliff responded, thinking it out. 'We might manage it for a while, but after that we'd be like a fly on a straight wall, the difference being we'd fall off and drop into the depths where a fly would not. What I am thinking is that the monsters that have appeared have probably come up this chasm side, perhaps driven out indeed by the discharge of volcanic gas and fire. There are none in this cavern here, so they must have come from deep below.'

'And we must go down there and find out,' the geologist remarked. 'Do you suggest we climb down?'

Cliff looked about him and presently began a slow tour of exploration. When he came to a five-foot depression in the rock-strewn cavern floor he pointed to it.

'We go down in the bore,' he announced, 'and we start from this depression. It's comfortably deep enough with the ridged edge to tilt our nose sufficiently. Come — we'll be on our way.'

They trooped back into the machine and closed the airlock. When their helmets and cylinders were removed, Cliff returned to the switchboard, turned the machine about and then drove it gently over the edge of the five-foot depression. As he had expected, the outer casing tilted nose downward so that it was obliquely directed towards the canyon.

'So far, so good,' he commented. 'Now we start to bore to the lower levels, which is the equivalent of going down into the chasm.'

He moved the drill-selector lever, gave the engines three-quarter power and then engaged the gears. From outside, the din muffled by the insulated walls, there came the scream of the spinning drill as it bit into the rocks, shattering them into dust in an area wide enough to take the full bulk of the bore. Gradually the vessel began to descend, the powdered rock being carried to the rear of the machine there to be blasted into nothing by the disintegrator chambers.

Silent, everybody watched the mirror with its reflected scene of ever-approaching rock that crumbled as the drill ate through it. The depth gauge crept higher. 300 feet, 400 feet — 500 feet.

'Are you sure,' Joan asked presently, 'that we'll come out at the floor of that chasm? Suppose we misfire and go below that point? You're only working to guesswork, after all.'

'We're bound to emerge either high up the chasm or else on the floor of it,' Cliff replied. 'I didn't allow for it being any more than four hundred feet down. We'll come through in a while.'

Rather too suddenly, as events proved. A few moments later, when the gauge was registering 580 feet, the bore found itself with no more rock to penetrate. The machine had emerged diagonally out of the chasm side. Instantly Cliff cut the power and then raised the shutters from the windows. Crowding around them the party stared down on to a much nearer view of the phosphorescent underworld.

'We're not exactly in a happy position,'

Dr. Blair said anxiously. 'We're balanced half over the edge of this ledge, Brooks. A fraction further and we'll drop.'

Cliff settled at the switchboard again, threw the mechanism into reverse and allowed the tractor claws to pull the opposite way. Accordingly the bore withdrew until it was safely balanced. Behind it loomed the perfect shaft it had made on its journey down.

'Now what?' Martin Dagman questioned. 'Do we finish the descent by the natural process of mountaineering?'

'Too dangerous,' Cliff replied. 'That glow down there may be a sea of molten metal for all we know.'

'Unlikely,' remarked Colin Naysmith. 'If prehistoric monsters came from down there it can't be molten. My guess is some natural volcanic light.'

'Whatever the answer we're still going to use the bore,' Cliff decided. 'I'll use the radar detector and see if we can get an echo back from the bottom of the chasm, then we'll know how far we have yet to go.'

He moved the levers and buttons on

the control board, and outside the vessel a long boom arm began to project from the nose just clear of the drill. Finally, at the limit of its extension, it was fifty feet beyond the edge of the chasm. Cliff adjusted the radar device on the end of the rod by remote control beams, and then switched on the current. On the detector screen an echo presently flashed back along the line calibrated at 300 feet.

'Another three hundred feet down,' he announced. 'Right! Now I can calculate things properly.'

With the electronic computer he worked out exactly the angle of the diagonal the machine would have to take to emerge comfortably at the chasm floor, and once this was done the thing was easy. He withdrew the bore for half a mile, tilted it to a sharper angle, then again set the drill in action. Once more the astonishing iron mole was on its way, and once more the party watched the screen, the windows remaining shuttered whilst the vessel moved so no rock could cause splintering.

580 feet — 600 feet — 700 feet — So

at length to the required 900 feet without any diminution in progress. The rocks were only of the normal granite and marble variety, according to the geologist, and simple enough to break. So, with a final jerk, the bore emerged once again, its screw screaming in emptiness.

Cliff switched off and unshuttered the windows. In silence he, Joan and the scientists gazed — and still gazed. The distance and angle had been perfectly estimated, for they had crept out of a vast rock cliff on to a floor of whitish pumice rock. They were in a cavern of staggering dimensions, from the walls of which spouted great jets of natural fire, some of it green with copper basis, some of it yellow, some pale blue. The combination of all the lot produced a steady white light, since when one mass of flame was inoperative another was at its peak. The general effect was of ghostly moonlight illuminating this weird, empty land nearly a thousand feet below surface.

'Interesting, but not very impressive,' Blair said at length. 'Your molten sea turns out to be pumice dust lighted by volcanic fire, Brooks.'

Cliff nodded. 'I'm wondering if there's an explanation for that rumbling I heard when I looked down here at first. Let's see if it's still present.'

He switched on the exterior microphone and almost immediately there came the growling rumble of either water, rushing wind, or something in violent motion.

'Keep the machine going,' Blair advised. 'We might as well explore now we've got this far.'

Cliff nodded and, with the windows still unshuttered, he drove the machine slowly along the cavern floor, noting in awed silence the immensity of this underworld and the columns of pumice rock, seared by terrific volcanic heat, which supported the weight of the rock overhead. In many ways, the scene reminded him of a lunar landscape, Overhead everything was totally black, but in all other directions it loomed starkly white under the multicoloured pulses of light.

'Look!' Martin Dagman exclaimed suddenly, pointing. 'If that isn't a dinosaur I'm crazy!'

There was no doubt about it. A monstrous brute of the prehistoric era had suddenly come into view in the distance, prowling amidst the rocks. It caught sight of the approaching bore and halted, probably astounded at this new creature invading its territory.

'There's something very queer here,' Colin Naysmith observed, his lean face pensive. 'These monsters just could not exist in a land like this full of barren rockery with no water, no flesh to eat. It's an established fact that the dinosaurs lived in an age of sticky heat, lush vegetation and copious moisture. The carnivorous ones were cannibalistic — if I may say so — and often slew one another so they could eat. The herbivorous ones, like the iguanodon, ate trees and bushes. Only one answer to it, there must be a region here somewhere which is true Jurassic, where they live as normally as they did eighty million years ago.'

'Just what animal is that?' asked Joan.

'A brontosaurus,' the expert replied. 'One of the less fierce types of monsters and weighing about thirty or forty tons at full maturity — '

He was drowned out at that moment, as through the microphone there came a scream from the brontosaurus. It was a yell of fear, not fury. Swinging round it began to bolt through the rocky distances.

'Follow it!' Naysmith urged quickly. 'It will probably lead us to wherever these monsters have their home — '

Cliff promptly put on speed, driving the rumbling machine at a good thirty-five miles an hour, which was a deal faster than the scared brontosaurus could travel. There was a vision of its enormous rear heaving and jolting as it panicked its way onward, until at length it turned a corner. Cliff kept hot on the trail, speeding past the huge pillars of pumice rock, then very suddenly the cavern began to narrow down as he turned the corner in the wake of the monster. There was a narrow tunnel ahead, or at least it seemed narrow after the immensity of the cavern, and at the end of it was more white light.

'Do I keep going?' he demanded. 'There's just enough width for the bore to get along — '

'Certainly you keep going!' The expert on prehistory was peering through the window. 'This is the way the bronto went. Maybe we're arriving at some sensible solution to all this mystery.'

Cliff slowed down and switched on the searchlights. The tunnel ahead was empty, so evidently the monster had escaped through the opening at the far end. In a matter of two minutes the bore had reached it, gone beyond it and into a region as different from the rocky cavern as anything that could be imagined.

'I'll be damned!' Blair exclaimed frankly. 'This is something I never hoped to see! Look at it!'

It was a needless injunction. Cliff stopped the machine and, with Joan at his side and the scientists crowded round the windows, he looked upon something lifted wholesale from the Jurassic Age. Here there was an underworld so enormous it was impossible to tell that it was not on the surface, except for the blackness of the 'sky'. Volcanic gases lighted a land of swamps, the residue of dispersed volcanic steam, of monster ferns, of palm-like cycads and conifers. Everywhere there was this dense jungle, yet nowhere a flowering plant or a sign of grass. Everything was big, and rank, and overpowering. Here and there in the distance was the shape of a vast reptilian head, or the towering back of a prowling dinosaur. In the swamps, too, life was moving, life once again on a gigantic pattern.

'The Jurassic Age, perfectly preserved,' Martin Dagman exclaimed in rapture. 'Dangerous it may be, but I think we ought to go outside and take a look at it.'

'With monsters of that size looming around?' Blair asked dubiously.

'We can take the risk. At least I'm going to. I don't know about the rest of you, but I'm going to photograph this lot.'

'Better see how the atmosphere is first,' Cliff cautioned. 'And don't forget that our primary purpose here is to stop nitrogene gas — '

'Our primary purpose, yes,' Naysmith agreed, 'but Dr. Blair, Dagman and myself are here solely for scientific recording. I'm willing to go outside as well — How's the atmosphere?'

Cliff looked at the instrument board. 'High percentage of nitrogene,' he announced. 'Enough, I'd say, to make us atavise quite a lot if we breathe too much of it. Temperature's on one hundred and six.'

'Normal enough for this slice of prehistoric land,' Naysmith said, 'but we're going to find it plenty hot. Volcanic origin, no doubt. High percentage of nitrogene, eh? That seems to prove more than ever that nitrogene is definitely the main reason for these beasts surviving.'

'What is puzzling me,' Joan remarked, 'is how this land survived the recent volcanic upheaval. It doesn't look as though it has even been touched.'

'Probably it wasn't.' Cliff surveyed it again. 'The volcanic fire went straight up the chasm from the cavern we've just come from. It wouldn't touch this region at all.'

'How do you account for the pterodactyls and other beasts leaving this paradise of theirs to explore the upper world?'

'Curiosity,' answered Naysmith. 'The

uppermost instinct in any living creature — even humans. Finding the way to the surface open, a thing that has never happened before, the monsters and birds went on the prowl. Nothing more in it than that. They also found nitrogene gas at the surface which was all they needed to keep them comfortable.'

'One might add the impetus of instinct,' Joan murmured to Cliff. 'Maybe they sensed somehow that Herbert was above.'

Cliff was not sure of the answer to this one, so he let the matter drop.

'We'd better change into tropical rig and helmets,' he said. 'Then we'll take a look about us.'

It was half an hour before the party was ready, having changed into clothes almost Grecian in their brevity. About their waists they carried instruments and flame-guns, and upon their backs were the oxygen cylinders leading to the helmets. They were ready for exploration — the scientists to more closely study the Jurassic life, and Cliff to determine where the nitrogene gas was coming from.

Blair opened the airlock and stepped out to the soft, spongy soil. The atmosphere was exactly like that of a very humid conservatory — sticky, cloying warmth with a heavy preponderance of water vapour.

'Grand place to grow orchids,' Naysmith remarked, grinning — then he began to follow Blair as he led the way, sinking over the ankles at every step in sloppy, tepid ooze.

'Our limit of distance from the bore will be two miles,' Cliff cautioned, playing out a thin steel wire as he went. 'And this is our only link with it. If the wire gets broken heaven help us.'

The others nodded briefly, too interested in surveying the cycads and conifers to speculate on the dangers. To Cliff and Joan the surroundings were only of secondary consideration: Cliff was busy reading his instruments for registering nitrogene gas, and Joan watched with him. Not that she understood anything about the matter, but because she liked sharing in the business.

'Look,' Naysmith muttered presently,

halting. 'How's that for a turtle?'

The monstrous amphibian was only visible for a moment as it waddled into the undergrowth, but it was certainly every inch of twenty feet across the shell.

'I never thought turtles existed in the Jurassic Age,' Joan commented as they went on again.

'Definitely they did,' Naysmith told her. 'Turtles, snakes, lizards, tortoises, crocodiles. They all existed, but on a far bigger scale than the present day varieties. You know, Mr. Brooks, I'm never going to be able to thank you enough for giving me a chance to see all this!'

The immense enthusiasm of the scientists was obvious. Cliff, though, was not in the least enthusiastic. He feared every moment that a dinosaur would present itself and perhaps crush the life out of them, or if not that, snap the vital steel wire which led back as a lifeline to the bore. However, the lost Jurassic area was of immense extent and the monsters were evidently fairly sparse. Certainly none came close enough to cause trouble though they were several times glimpsed through the trees. By the time the two-mile limit of the steel wire had been reached Blair made an observation.

'Same thing down here as up above. Every animal is female. You notice that, Naysmith?'

The lanky scientist nodded. 'Yes; and I'm wondering how the devil the race keeps going. We've seen about ten females and no males. It doesn't make sense.'

'The answer, according to my theory, is that some disease has wiped out the males,' Blair responded. 'I outlined that to Mr. Brooks some time ago. It does happen in species many a time: one sex or the other contracts a fatal malady and in the end that, of course, means the extinction of the species in its entirety because there are no progeny. That would seem to have happened here. The females are going on living because they have such a colossal life span — but there are no new additions. And never can be.'

'Unless Herbert — ' Joan started to say, and then checked herself.

'Herbert?' Blair looked puzzled. 'I believe you have made reference to that

139

name before, Mrs. Brooks. Might I ask — '

'Look out!' Dagman interrupted, and just in time he and the rest of the party flung themselves sideways out of harm's reach as a snake, thicker than a man's body, came gliding down the bole of a nearby conifer. Cliff took immediate advantage of the interruption to stop all questioning concerning Herbert.

'Have you gentlemen seen all you wish?' he asked. 'Our wire is at the limit and I have determined all I need to know regarding nitrogene.'

'Yes,' Naysmith said grudgingly, 'I suppose there's nothing more we need here. Have you got all the film you want Dagman?'

'I'll make it do, though I'd like to stop here for about a year and photograph everything in sight — Yes, we'd better get back.'

Since wisdom was prevailing over curiosity Cliff did not delay in leading the way back to the bore. He and Joan went on ahead, the scientists bringing up the rear and arguing amongst themselves upon the various evidences they had seen.

'Did you mean it when you said you'd learned all you want about nitrogene?' Joan asked in surprise.

'No. I said it so we can get back to the bore. It just doesn't dawn on these scientific geniuses how dangerous it is to be out here without adequate protection. There's a great deal yet that I want to know about nitrogene and its source, but we'll do it from the safety of the bore, thank you.'

Once within the machine, Cliff waited until the three scientists had entered, and then Blair glanced enquiringly.

'What now, Mr. Brooks? Your mission isn't yet accomplished, is it, even if ours is?'

'I'm going to trace the source of that rumbling we can hear so constantly,' Cliff answered. 'I think it may have something to do with the nitrogene gas — possibly the blowhole from which the gas is emanating. We'll use the bore for a little exploration and see what we can locate.'

'Excellent idea!' Naysmith exclaimed, and Dagman quickly unfastened his camera and put in a fresh cassette of film.

Settling at the switchboard Cliff started up the power plant, engaged the tractors, and then set the machine on the move. With a certain irresistible force it ploughed through the midst of the undergrowth, smashing down the smaller trees as it advanced. Certainly there was no longer anything to be feared from the monsters. Here and there one of them came in view, saw the bore approaching, and promptly turned and ran. Mechanisation was something new in this forgotten land.

Ever and again Cliff stopped and listened to the microphone connected to the exterior. Only by this means could he judge whether or not the vessel was advancing in the direction of the mystery noise. At length it became evident that the sound was much louder — like a not-far distant Niagara — so Cliff kept on advancing steadily whilst Joan and the scientists remained at the windows, watching the fantastic trees and vegetation plunging over before the juggernaut's advance.

6

Vision of hell

It was nearly two hours later before the source of the noise was at last discovered. The bore came gradually out of the forest into a rocky region where obvious volcanic activity was in progress. Nearly a dozen geysers were jetting hot water nearly two hundred feet into the roof of the mighty cavern, and the noise of these, together with a sullenly bubbling lake of molten rock, combined to produce the constant roaring note so similar to that of a distant waterfall.

Cliff stopped the bore once again and sat gazing through the window on to the rocky wilderness.

'I think this is the spot we're looking for,' he said. 'If all this volcanic upheaval can go on here it's a fair certainty that the nitrogene gas has its exit here, too. I want to make a few tests before going any further — so fix up something for us to eat, Joan, will you, whilst I get busy?'

Joan nodded and turned actively to her task. Dagman put his camera to his eye and panned it slowly to take in the full scene. Naysmith scribbled notes industriously. Cliff for his part put on his helmet, strapped his belt about his waist, and then adjusted his air cylinder on his back.

'I've got to take the risk,' he explained as Joan gave him a worried glance. 'This detector of mine will show where the seat of nitrogene is. Once I have that I can work out the rest.'

He opened the airlock and stepped outside. Into the control room came the screaming din of the geyser, as ear-splitting as the safety valves on a dozen old-time locomotives. Cliff could never have endured it had he not switched off the external pick-up in his helmet. This made things quite silent, and he was able to concentrate detachedly upon his task.

He wandered a good deal amongst the rocks, consulting his detector at intervals. When at length he returned to the control room he was looking reasonably satisfied.

When he had shut the airlock and had his helmet removed he summed up his investigation over much-needed food.

'The detector shows a tremendous pressure of nitrogene in the region of those higher rocks there,' he announced, nodding through the window. 'You can't tell from here, but actually they are like fine honeycombs and gas is coming out of them at gale force. This detector' — he held it up — 'shows pressure distribution in the same way as a barometer, so it didn't take me so very long to find what I was looking for.'

'And now what?' Blair asked. 'Block up the honeycomb rock?'

Cliff shook his head and swallowed some tea. 'That would only cause the gas to blow out somewhere else, I'm afraid. I'm going to get to its very roots — if one can say that about a gas — and divert into some other channel that normally carries away volcanic discharge. That was my original idea, and I may as well stick to it.'

'And how do we find the source?' Naysmith asked. 'Sounds impossible to me.'

'I propose to take radar soundings. That gas must be coming up a shaft. Right?'

'Presumably,' Naysmith admitted, but Dagman, the geologist, gave a vehement nod.

'No doubt whatever of that.'

'Very well, then. I'm going to drive the bore downwards from this point, parallel with the shaft that contains the nitrogene, and we can tell whether or not we're still following the shaft by means of the radar echoes. If the radar beams hit against the shaft wall — where there is hollow space beyond — they give only a weak signal. If they strike solid rock they give a strong signal. It's as simple as that.'

'You mean,' Blair asked, thinking, 'that by that means we can constantly know whether we're still near the shaft or not?'

'Exactly. We use a similar method in deep mining when we are testing out old blowholes. It's simply a scientific version of tapping an apparent solid to see whether it's hollow or solid inside. I have no idea,' Cliff finished, 'how far this shaft may go down, and if anybody here would rather be taken home before I — '

'Nonsense,' Blair said brusquely. 'The

lower we go the better, and I think I speak for all of us here, except your wife, of course.'

'Wherever Cliff goes, I go too,' Joan shrugged.

'Very well, then.' Cliff ate for a while and then added: 'I cannot help thinking that it will take us to the very core of volcanic activity, and that may prove no picnic. However since we've started the job we may as well finish it.'

The meal was finished somewhat soberly. So far the expedition had proved exciting and interesting, besides clearing up many problems of the prehistoric ages. But the next stage was something very different — a plunge into unknown depths, into the vice of ever-increasing heat and pressure.

'Do we need rest yet or shall we start?' Cliff asked when the meal was over. The vote was that they start, so Cliff once more took up his position at the controls, closed the window shutters, and then drove the bore forward to the spot he had preselected.

It was a volcanic depression in the ground,

a hollow about twelve feet in depth and reasonably near enough to the nitrogene gas rock-sponge for his purpose.

The outer casing of the bore tilted sharply, the drill tip hitting the base of the depression. Cliff switched on the rotary screw to half-rev, and so the descent began, volcanic rock spinning into powder as the bore relentlessly drove downwards. The depth gauge, which had formerly stood at just over 900 feet, rapidly rose to 1,000. Cliff turned to the radar apparatus and switched it on, 'fishing' for direction until at length he had the screen responding to his liking. The 'echo' was definitely weak as it deflected back from the inner wall of the nitrogene gas shaft.

'Of course,' Dagman remarked, lounging comfortably in his chair, 'we've only scratched the very thin outer skin of our planet as yet. A thousand feet is neither here nor there! Now, if we were down a thousand miles we'd really have something to enthuse about.'

'Maybe we shall be before we're finished,' Cliff remarked briefly, watching the radar screen.

'A thousand miles!' Naysmith exclaimed. 'The bore won't stand it, will it? Think of the pressure at that depth!'

'It'll stand it all right. Ask Dr. Blair: he saw the outer shell metal tested under the strains equalling those that are computed to exist near the Earth's centre.'

'That's right,' Blair confirmed. 'The metal stood up to it magnificently. Just the same, a thousand miles is a bit of a stretch, Brooks. You don't believe the gas core can be that low down, do you?'

'Not far short of it maybe. Volcanoes have their roots hundreds of miles inside the Earth, don't forget. I'm pretty well prepared for anything.'

The others said no more. They watched the prismatic screen for a time, but since it only gave a perpetual view of rock being destroyed by the ever-whirring drill, they finally grew tired of the monotony and dozed off to sleep. Even Joan found herself drowsing. When she awoke again Cliff was still at the switchboard, but the depth gauge had shifted from the foot measure to the mile scale. It read 15 miles.

'How are we doing?' Joan dragged herself into wakefulness in the stuffy atmosphere and glanced at the recumbent scientists in their chairs.

'Very nicely.' Cliff yawned behind his hand. 'The radar says we're still parallel to the nitrogene shaft and, as you can see, we've gone down fifteen miles. So far we haven't hit against any really hard rock. If we do, the drill may have to be changed or else the revs increased. Think you can take over whilst I grab some rest?'

'Well, I — ' Joan looked anxious. 'What do I have to do?'

'Nothing much. The course is already set and the bore will keep on going downwards as long as the power plant runs. All you have to do is see the plant does keep running — and if you hit on something which stops the machine, cut off the power at once or the drill may be chewed to bits! Also, if you see a signal twice as powerful on that radar screen wake me at once. Right?'

'Right,' Joan acknowledged, and slid into the seat that Cliff vacated.

How long he slept he did not know, but

when he awakened it was to find that the scientists were also awake again, watching the screen, talking, and making notes.

'Everything in order?' Cliff asked, getting up and looking at the gauge.

'Aye, aye, sir,' Joan smiled. 'We're making quite high speed considering. One hundred and six miles down and nothing stopping us.'

'Good. Our speed is because we have gravity to help us. We'll be a lot slower going up again — '

'Why?' Naysmith asked, puzzled. 'We've cleared a shaft for ourselves all the way to the surface, haven't we? Our rubble is destroyed in the rear. The rear-mirrors show a diagonal tunnel stretching away behind us. Why can't we follow that in order to get home? Be much easier than boring through new rock.'

'It all depends on where we finish up,' Cliff replied. 'If we can follow the same course home we will, of course. Okay Joan, I'll take over again. Fix another meal for us, will you?'

So it went on, a seemingly endless round of meals, sleep; and time to study the situation. The clock alone kept track of the days and nights on the surface. Then, at four hundred miles depth the bore broke free of the solid rock and crashed a good forty feet to the floor of a cavern. The impact was terrific and, despite the outer shell, those within the control room were flung to the floor with painful force.

Cliff got up slowly, rubbing his aching shoulder, and helped Joan to rise beside him. He switched off the power plant and trained the searchlights upon the cavern into which they had fallen. It was apparently deserted, a titanic catacomb of the world four hundred miles below the light of day. Unlighted and never before seen by living beings.

'This the place we want?' Naysmith asked, peering through the temporarily unshuttered window. 'Pretty awe-inspiring mausoleum, isn't it?'

'It's only a deep rock cavern,' Cliff replied presently, looking at the radar screen. 'That further wall we can see over there is still the wall of the nitrogene gas shaft. We have to still keep going.'

'And I think,' Dagman said looking outside intently, 'that you will find a change of drill necessary from here on. The rock formation of this cavern floor is very different from that of its roof, which is probably why the cavern is here. Most caverns are caused by the parting of two different types of rock. They don't hold together.'

'Thanks for the tip.' Cliff started up the plant again. 'We'll soon know. I'm carrying on from that dip over there.'

He headed the bore towards it and, as usual, the nose dipped into the cavity. But this time the drill screamed fiendishly without producing much result. The rock formation was different and exceptionally tough.

Grim-faced, Cliff increased the revs to maximum, but still he made little impression — so he changed to the second drill, and to his relief there was an instant result. The bore began to descend once again, moving much more slowly now, tearing its way through rock pulverised to unthinkable hardness by the ever-increasing pressures that would reach their maximum at the nickel-iron core of Earth itself. Through this nothing could penetrate.

The temperature began rising. So far it had remained fairly consistently around the eighty mark, but with this incursion into the still deeper realms and correspondingly greater nearness to fires in the bowels of the world, the mercury began a slow climb. After half an hour it had reached ninety — and two hours later it was touching the hundred mark. Thirsty, perspiring copiously, the party watched the prismatic screen for some sign of something interesting.

They were left unrewarded, so far. 425 miles — 500 miles. And at length 650miles. Then the machine stopped dead! The temperature was 106 degrees Fahrenheit.

'Now what?' Naysmith asked anxiously. 'Don't tell me the power's failed!'

'No. We've struck something even tougher.'

'And at this depth I can make a good guess what it is,' Dagman said. 'We must by now be on the outer perimeter of the monstrous nickel-iron centre of the

Earth. We've hit the first ultra-hard substance and it's going to be a miracle if we can penetrate it. Far as my geologic knowledge goes we ought by now to be at the point where all volcanic fire has its source — including nitrogene gas. Does the radar still say we're following the shaft?'

'Yes. But I agree with you, Dagman, it's time we'd hit bottom — '

Cliff switched the drills, this time the toughest of them all — number three drill. He switched the plant on again, and to the accompaniment of a good deal of jolting the bore at last began to move again.

'Whew!' Joan murmured in relief. 'Thank heaven for that. Does it occur to you, Cliff, that if we get jammed whilst we are in the midst of rock we just can't get back? Be no room to turn the machine around.'

'I know,' he muttered. 'Don't even think about such things!'

From here on progress was extremely slow, and at times it looked as though the drill was going to fail, even though it was on maximum revs and the plant running full blast. Then again the jerk, and further progress.

The depth gauge read 780 miles when the bore abruptly fell from the midst of imprisoning rock and crashed down the steep slope of some kind of mountainside. The outer casing tumbled over and over, the effect to those within the inner shell being one of tremendous concussions and vibration. They were pitched helplessly around the control room, knocked off their feet as soon as they struggled to them — until at last the onslaught ceased as the bore came to rest.

Aching, especially where bones had only just healed, Cliff fought his way to his feet and crept to the switchboard. He cut off the power and then glanced through the window. He saw a vision that looked as though it had come straight out of hell. There seemed to be fire everywhere. But there was not the time now to dwell upon it. Turning, he dragged Joan to her feet, and she dabbed painfully at a vicious cut over her left eyebrow.

One by one the scientists also rose, and

for the next ten minutes the first aid kit worked overtime as bruises and cuts were attended to — then a general move to the windows was made.

'It's awe-inspiring!' Blair whispered. 'There just isn't any other word for it! Awe-inspiring.'

Dagman panned his camera for a space.

The scene outside was quite hypnotic in its unholy fascination, painted entirely in flame red. There were mighty cliffs, down which flowed Niagaras of molten metal, boiling rivers of lava plunging into depthless chasms. From the chasms arose clouds of thick, woolly smoke all drifting away through natural blowholes in the rocks. Monstrous buttresses of black rock stood isolated amongst the flowing tides of hell. Here and there a promontory like a pointing finger stabbed out over a chasm and looked as though it would over balance into the depths.

'If this isn't the domain of Old Nick I don't know what is,' Naysmith observed, mopping his face. 'Stretches as far as the eye can see, too. You don't suggest going any lower Brooks do you?'

'No need,' Cliff replied, turning aside to look at the radar detector. 'We're no longer following the nitrogene shaft. This is where the nitrogene evidently comes from, produced amongst these volcanic vapours and gases.'

'And we've got to trace it?' Joan asked.

'If possible, and then divert it. It'll be a long job and take some figuring out, but it must be done.'

Silence. Then Blair took his gaze from the awesome vision to make a remark.

'I'm quite sure, as Dagman was earlier, that we're now on the very perimeter of Earth's core. This molten condition will probably continue for many hundreds of miles lower yet until it ceases by very reason of the unthinkable pressure existing at the centre of the Earth.'

'Possibly so,' Cliff agreed, 'but that side of it doesn't interest us — fortunately. We've come as far as we dare. My next job is to start finding the exact source of nitrogene with my instruments and then work out how to divert it. First, though, I think an examination of the bore's exterior is called for. We came down this mountain face, or whatever it is, with the devil of a hammering. The rest of you coming outside with me?'

There were glances again towards the seething hell, but nobody refused to accept the challenge. Inside ten minutes, Cliff in the lead in his helmet and brief costume, the party was scrambling out of the airlock to the rocks. They were immediately conscious of the suffocating heat and heady sense of pressures, but thanks to their helmets and oxygen tanks were able to breathe freely enough.

Blair, Naysmith, and Dagman investigated the nose of the bore, whilst Cliff examined the rear — and the more he examined the more troubled he became. The bore had certainly suffered in its fall down the cliff face, to the extent of having the main driving rod of the tractor belts broken in two.

'But that's our only means of motive power!' Joan cried in horror through her microphone. 'It can be repaired, can't it?'

'I hope so,' Cliff muttered, and he

motioned the others to him. Grim-faced they inspected the smashed master-bar.

'I don't like it,' Naysmith said worriedly. 'Joining a bar which has to take such terrific strain is an impossibility. Our only chance is to forge a new one, and how are we going to do it?'

'Plainly we can't,' Cliff replied. 'What I think we'll have to do is make a union to hold the broken ends in place and then weld the whole thing into one piece. It ought to hold. Following back the track we've made to get down here we'll have very little resistance to encounter — nothing more than a perpetual steep gradient. If we had solid rock to penetrate we'd never do it.'

'I agree that a union would probably hold the bar once we're in the tunnel for the return trip,' Blair commented. 'But how do we get up to the tunnel? Look where we came through!'

He pointed overhead and the party strained their necks to look at the towering escarpment painted by the flickering red glow. Some two hundred feet up the craggy wall was an irregular hole, looking like the entrance to a cave, and it was from that spot that the bore had fallen upon entering this satanic region.

'That is the problem,' Blair insisted. 'We just can't get the bore up that escarpment with the tractor bar joined only by a union. It'd snap right away.'

It took several moments for each one in the party to comprehend that they were completely ditched. Even driving straight forwards into the rock face, then slowly curving upwards until the original tunnel was reached, was not practical either. A union repair job would not hold out under such terrific pressures.

Naysmith glanced at the bore pensively, then shook his head.

The idea had been in the back of his mind that perhaps if all the men pushed and Joan sat at the controls — No, the gradient was too steep. Only a powerful winch and hawser would be able to supply the extra pull necessary to safeguard the union until the tunnel was gained.

'Well, we're not beaten yet,' Cliff said finally. 'We'll think of something. In the meantime I'm going to try and finish the job I came for. Doesn't seem much point in your coming with Joan and me, gentlemen. Perhaps you'd get busy with the equipment and manufacture a union clamp. We've got to be knowing what it can do.'

'We'll do that,' Blair assented promptly. 'I know just what's needed.' He jerked his helmeted head to the two scientists and led the way back inside the machine. Cliff took Joan's arm and began to lead her carefully amongst the rocks.

'You don't have to hide anything from me, Cliff,' she said quietly, as they progressed. 'What are the prospects?'

'Mighty dim! I'd be a fool to say otherwise. One can't push a thing as heavy as the bore as one would a motor car.'

'But — But we can't stay here, Cliff! It's unthinkable!'

'What other proposition is there? Walk back up the tunnel for seven hundred and eighty miles? I don't doubt we could do that in time, but what about food and the nitrogene gas that must be leaking up that

162

shaft we've made? Our air cylinders wouldn't hold out. It's a nasty position whichever way we look at it.'

It was plain from Joan's expression behind her helmet that she could not take the situation in. It was altogether grim. So instead she turned her attention to surveying the surroundings. Every step she and Cliff took was dangerous. At any moment the rocky plateau on which they and the bore stood might dissolve under the corroding influence of the eternal fires below. They felt like a couple of beings on the brink of Dante's 'Inferno'.

'Just look at it!' Cliff said at last as they came to the edge of the major chasm into which the 'waterfall' of molten fire was cascading. 'Was there ever a sight like that?'

Joan could only shake her head dumbly. The chasm, as near as they dared look into it, was a raging fire. The noise of its eternal fury was like muffled thunder. From it were belching gases and smoke in endless, woolly clouds. Cliff found himself wondering how long they would last without their masks, then he gave a nudge for the exploration to continue.

Ever and again Cliff consulted his detector and as a towering cliff was approached he snapped his fingers in delight.

'That's it!' he exclaimed excitedly. 'The base of the shaft which is carrying the nitrogene to the surface. Now, let's take a good look.'

He lifted the binoculars to his eyes and focussed them on the smoke-enshrouded rock at the base of the cliff. Joan watched him, lying limply against a boulder and fanning herself as heat blasted in upon her from every side.

'It's pretty clear how the gas gets up there,' Cliff remarked at length. 'The underside of that cliff has that many holes in it, it looks like a colander! The gas evidently goes through them, drawn by draught, and escapes to the surface. A lot more of it must be dissipated down here, too, but that doesn't matter. We've got to stop it going up that particular shaft and divert it elsewhere.'

'For instance?' Joan asked wearily.

'That takes sorting out.' Cliff had the

glasses to his eyes again. 'There seems to be one gigantic cauldron of volcanic matter below, and the attendant smoke and gases. They are escaping up several shafts as well as this particular one that worries us. The best answer to that one is to block the shaft we're worried about and let the gas go where it will afterwards. Every one of these other vents must belong to a volcano somewhere on the surface — '

He lowered the glasses, perspiration pouring down his body in streams. Glancing at Joan he saw that she too was in a similar condition.

'Better get to the bore before we melt,' he said briefly. 'We'll discuss the matter there where it'll be a bit more comfortable.'

They made the return journey cautiously, and at length entered the bore after Blair had opened the airlock to them. He shut it behind them as they took off their helmets.

'To keep out the gases,' he explained. 'The gauge there shows there's a good deal of nitrogene, argon, and chlorine fumes, all deadly poison — ' He drew a bare forearm over his streaming forehead. 'Well, how did you make out?'

'Fairly well. We'll discuss it afterwards.' Cliff laid his helmet aside. 'My anxiety is chiefly for the bore. Are you getting on with that Union?'

Blair nodded. 'Naysmith and Dagman are hard at it in the tool chamber, and I've been helping them. We ought to have the union made in a couple of hours, then we can try our hand at welding it into place.'

'And if it fails to do as we hope?' Joan asked.

The scientist shrugged. 'If it fails, it seems to me it's the finish — and, candidly, I cannot see the master-bar having enough strength to pull us up the cliff face. In normal circumstances we wouldn't have much difficulty because the acclivity which leads to our entrance hole isn't too terribly steep.'

'Joan is of the opinion that it might be better to try and walk home than die here.' Cliff brooded for a moment. 'I wish that were somehow possible.'

'It would be if we were like the Jurassic monsters,' Blair sighed. 'Like the camel, they can go for days and weeks on end without food and water, storing it all inside them and regurgitating it when needed. Most useful.'

Shaking his head to himself he wandered out of the control room to the adjoining tool chamber. Cliff made several notes concerning his exploration outside, and then he followed in the scientist's wake. Joan, too, presently followed him and stood in the doorway of the tool chamber watching the tungsten steel union being moulded in the small atomic furnace. In thirty more minutes the thing was cast, and had only to cool, which was the signal for the party to return into the control room and settle to a meal.

'Y'know, I've been thinking about our predicament,' Naysmith commented, between bites of food. 'Maybe it isn't so serious as it looks. We've got radio equipment. What's to prevent us radioing to the surface for help? A new bore can easily be made to the design of this one, and within a month or less we could probably be rescued. All the rescuers have to do is follow the tunnel we've made.'

Cliff relaxed with a smile of relief. 'Now why on earth didn't I think of that? The perfectly obvious solution! Maybe I had that gas business too much on my mind. Congratulations, Naysmith! You've saved the day.'

He grinned like a schoolboy and went on eating.

'Just the same,' Blair said, 'we'll get the master-bar repaired as near as possible. We're going to take this bore back home if we can manage it. Too valuable to lose — And how about the gas, Brooks? What did you discover?'

Cliff gave the details and then exhibited the notes he had made.

'I've been making a few calculations, working them out from our position inside the Earth, the journey we took to follow the shaft, our direction according to the Earth's magnetic centre, and so forth. I believe it's a reasonable assumption that we have around us here the roots of many surface volcanoes. By closing that nitrogene gas vent we'll stop it getting to the surface in Britain — and incidentally we'll kill off the Jurassic Age as well. Instead it will escape through one of the other vents into a natural volcanic channel, thereby being discharged from one or other of the volcanoes at the surface.'

'I follow that,' Blair said, 'but how do we block that shaft? We daren't risk blowing anything up because in this region that might start a volcanic shift and dissolve everything, us included, in an ocean of molten lava.'

'True enough,' Cliff agreed. 'This is my idea, crazy though it sounds. I noticed in studying the shaft wall — which looks like a cliff face, of course — that a little way up it there are further vent holes, natural cavities in the rock. They'll be about one hundred feet higher than the hole-ridden underside of the shaft up which the gas is passing.'

'Well?' Naysmith raised his sandy eyebrows.

'Suppose I went up to one of those high vent holes? There I would be able to actually get into the shaft. Those holes in the shaft side are as big as cave entrances.'

'And do what?' Dagman asked bluntly. 'Kill yourself?'

'No. Once I was across you could send the small winch over to me on the hawser, along with one of the crucibles that we use in the atomic furnace. Then, putting the crucible on the end of the windlass cable I could lower it — the crucible into the molten rock sea below and haul it up by the 'bucketful'. I would tip it down the shaft and it would inevitably solidify as it ran against the cooler rock. By degrees it would be thick enough to form over the holes in the base of the shaft and finally would block them completely in solid rock form. Simply a natural welding job on a giant scale.'

'And damnably dangerous.' Blair shook his head. 'You'd risk your life, or severe burns, doing a thing like that.'

'Not in a fireproof suit. We have several aboard. Joan saw to that.'

'That's right,' Joan nodded. 'I had no idea but what we might need them if we got involved in a fire.'

'Fire is right!' Naysmith whistled. 'How do you propose to get up to the caves in the first place?'

'By the simple process of climbing from the plateau. One hundred feet is not such a problem and there's plenty of rock to grab hold of. I'm pretty sure I could do it. Once I had, one of you would have to throw the hawser up to me and I'd secure it. I couldn't take the end of it with me. It would be too heavy. With that part fixed the rest would be easy — sending over the winch and crucible. I'd take a secondary rope with me to help things — I'm pretty sure,' Cliff finished, 'that I could do it. And once those vent holes are sealed with solidified rock they're likely to stay that way for a long time to come. As long as we need to be interested, anyway.'

'Well,' Blair said finally, 'it's up to you, after all. You are the man determined to stop this gas: we can only offer help and suggestions, and I still say you're taking your life in your hands. Anyway, are you sure you can do all that climbing? What about your broken bones?'

Cliff grinned. 'They knitted up long

ago, otherwise the doctors wouldn't have released me as they did. Modern calcium treatment makes short work of bone troubles, don't forget.'

'Mmm. Well, anyway, I'd suggest you sleep on it. It's fantastic and yet for that very reason it might be just the thing which would work.'

'Then that's settled,' Cliff said, getting up. 'Now let's see if anything can be done to radio to the surface.'

He settled at the instruments and tuned in the equipment. Then he intoned into the microphone: 'Clifford Brooks' expedition calling London. Come in, please.'

Silence. No, not a complete silence. There was a curious burring noise in the speaker, fading and waxing. Blair in particular listened to it, and his brows knitted.

'Calling London!' Cliff repeated. 'Can you hear me? Come in, please. Urgent!'

He frowned as still no reply came through; then he went to work with careful adjustments.

'I don't understand it,' he muttered.

172

'Everything's tuned in properly and there ought to be an answer — '

'But,' Blair put in sombrely, 'I don't think there will be. There's one point been overlooked. At this depth in the Earth we're also in the midst of the magnetic lines of force that Earth is always generating in her constant revolution. On the surface, or at a slight depth below, there is no interference — but here we're deeper than man has ever been. A direct cable would give us communication, but radio is out because of the magnetic interference. You hear that burring noise? Interpreted, that is the magnetism which is causing the trouble.'

Cliff stared, horrified. 'You — you mean there just isn't any way to get through?'

'That's my belief. Carry on trying if you want to, but I think it's a waste of time.'

Apparently Blair's deduction was correct, for though he fiddled with the control for nearly half an hour Cliff got no hint of an answer. Finally he gave up in disgust.

'Let's see how that union is,' he growled. 'Maybe it's set by now and we can try and help ourselves out.'

He led the way out of the control room, and the scientists and Joan followed him. The tungsten steel union was perfectly cooled, and in the testing block it resisted the maximum of pressures — as indeed it ought to do since it was cast in the hardest metal known to science.

'All right,' Blair said at length. 'We'd better get outside and see what can be done. Bring the welding tackle, Naysmith.'

Before long the menfolk were outside and hard at work on the fractured master-bar, encased in their helmets and with perspiration streaming from them as they toiled and struggled. Joan remained in the control room, the airlock shut. For one thing she had elected to clear the remains of the meal, and for another it would be her job to start up the power plant and so put the bar on test when it was welded. The signal for her to do this came an hour later. She looked through the main window and saw Cliff and the three scientists perched around the outer shell of the bore, the entire driving shaft exposed and bulging in the centre where the union had been heavily welded into position.

Cliff stood waiting and watching as Joan switched on the power plant and then, as previously instructed, engaged the driving mechanism at minimum speed. Her heart raced for joy as the bore began to move very slowly. She saw the group outside watching the master-bar with helmeted heads stooped forward.

'Holding so far,' came Blair's tense voice through his microphone. 'Have her increase speed.'

Cliff gave the necessary signals, and Joan obeyed. With sudden acceleration the bore began to travel around the plateau, turning gradually under Cliff's directions until it was facing that grim cliff escarpment which was the main barrier to an escape.

'Any reason why we shouldn't try making the climb now?' Cliff asked. 'At least we'll know how we stand, whether we're to make it or not.'

Blair reflected briefly, then: 'Okay. If the bar snaps we can only stop. We shan't slide backwards; the angle isn't steep enough. Yes, tell your wife.'

Cliff climbed back over the bore and swiftly wrote a note, holding it against the main window for Joan to read. She looked surprised, but finally nodded. Satisfied that she understood, Cliff returned to join the scientists, thereafter keeping his attention on the spinning bar with its sinister-looking joint.

In a matter of moments the bore reached the foot of the escarpment. Then it began to climb slowly over the rocks, creeping up gradually, rock by rock, tipping and jolting its outer casing so violently it took the scientists and Cliff all their time to hang on.

Further — slowly but surely — the exhaust jets roaring fiendishly to the rear. Cliff gave a worried glance above. That tunnel hole they needed seemed an appalling distance away — yet very gradually, like a drunken caterpillar, the bore lurched and crept higher and higher.

'Damn me, I do believe we're doing it!'

It was Naysmith's taut voice through his microphone. 'Taking it slowly, like this, we may yet manage to — '

He got no further. There was a sudden shattering crack that every man heard through his external earphones. A violent rattling followed, and loose ends of metal flew through the air. The bore stopped instantly, the root end of the master-bar whirling uselessly in a semicircle.

Cliff signalled frantically, and Joan, her face haggard, understood. The power plant stopped, and each man looked at the other. The effort had failed.

7

A thing of the past

'Well,' Blair said at last, 'at least we know where we stand. There just isn't a way to get this damned thing up the escarpment.'

'Better go inside and tell Joan,' Cliff muttered. 'As if she didn't know already.'

Morosely the four men returned inside the vessel, closing the airlock and pulling off their stuffy helmets. Joan's eyes were wide and anxious. She did not need to ask questions. She had seen quite enough, and the men's expressions were ample confirmation.

'Perhaps we'll think of something else yet,' Naysmith remarked, trying to grin, and the others looked at him moodily.

'Thanks for being so cheerful,' Cliff said, 'but to my mind we might as well resign ourselves to the fact that we're licked. I shall do the job I came for, which may at least help things back on the surface, and after that — ' He compressed his lips and shrugged. 'I dunno. Maybe we'd better get some sleep and see how things look then.'

Naturally, things did not look in the least different when the party awakened again. The bore was still where it had stopped, quarter way up the mountain face, and nobody had had any brilliant ideas in the interval.

'For the time being we forget it,' Cliff said as Joan rustled together some breakfast. 'At least I do. I'm setting about the job of sealing up that shaft and not giving attention to anything else. The rest of you will help me?'

'Naturally,' Blair responded, speaking as usual for the other two men. 'It will help to take our mind off things.'

So immediately after breakfast Cliff set forth, instruments strapped to him, together with a coil of rope. Joan, too, came with the scientists, all of them in their helmets. There was no point in her staying in the vessel, and that she was anxious about Cliff was plain to see.

He took his leave of her when he reached the towering cliff wall that was part of the nitrogene shaft. Then, watched anxiously by those below, he began his climb. At first it presented no difficulties to him because there were ample toe and finger holds, and at the moment he was only over the plateau. The real test of his nerve came when he began to edge leftwards, going higher all the time, until at length he was directly over the hell chasm from which the smoke and fumes were surging.

Ever and again he was lost to sight, and Joan's heart was in her mouth lest he had fallen, overpowered by the heat. But each time he came into view again, clinging like a fly to the rock face, edging upwards slowly but surely and taking care never to look downwards in case vertigo swept him to destruction.

He hardly knew himself how he had the courage and strength to make the climb. It was nothing more than determination to finish the task he'd set himself that got him through. And at last the lowest of the cave air holes was within reach. Panting desperately, for the oxygen cylinder only permitted a limited amount of air to reach his lungs, he hauled himself over the cave edge and struggled within. Then presently he stood up and waved to the remote figures visible through the smoke wreaths upon the plateau. The first and most difficult part of the job had been completed. He looked at the rope he had let fall loose on his journey. One end of it was anchored to a rock on the plateau, and the other end was in his hand as he triple knotted it round a rock spur. Here was his main contact between the plateau and himself.

Turning he moved into the cave until he came to the shaft itself. He peered into its depths and could distinctly make out the large red holes in the rocks through which the gas was passing, the flaming depths adding the ruby background. Yes, liquid rock poured down there should cure the trouble. Since the crucible he intended to use was made to stand up to a temperature nearly equal to that at the surface of the sun, he was quite satisfied that there would be no chance of the crucible melting due to the molten rock within it. Returning to the cave mouth he uncoiled the subsidiary rope from about his shoulder, noosed one end of it round the rope already stretching to the plateau, and so by gravity it slid down to the waiting hands of Blair.

'Okay for the winch!' Cliff yelled, amplifying his voice to maximum.

It was brought from the bore, together with other articles required, and fastened to the permanent rope by means of a pulley and hook. By pulling on the second rope, telphar wise, Cliff soon hauled the winch up to the cave mouth, and then repeated the process for the crucible and four hundred foot length of heat-resisting steel hawser.

This job done he pulled up the fireproof suit by the lifeline, scrambled into it and then went to work. All he had to do was fasten the crucible on the hawser and, using the winch, lower the crucible down the cliff face until it reached the dimly visible surface of the molten cauldron below — much the same as one might draw water from a well.

Up the crucible came, loaded to the brim with searing hot liquid rock. It sputtered and fizzed violently as Cliff manhandled it, but his fireproof suit was absolute protection for his actions. His eyes bright with triumph behind his helmet he watched the metal cascade in solidifying fire into the shaft, congealing as it went. The rock of the shaft was, of course, at a vastly lower temperature than the molten cauldron, producing almost instant solidification.

Cliff toiled for a couple of hours, sweating, struggling, resolutely determined to finish the job whilst he was about it. And he was finally rewarded by seeing the redness through the holes becoming less and less, until at last there was blackness. The sealing process was complete. Just for safe measure he drew up a further dozen 'buckets' of molten rock and thereby made sure that the job was thoroughly finished off.

Then he returned the winch, crucible and hawser to the plateau and finally used the pulley and hook to slide himself down. He landed heavily, the three scientists saving him from overbalancing.

'Done it?' Blair questioned.

'Absolutely. No gas will ever get through that shaft again — not until those rocks are blasted through with molten matter, anyway, and that isn't likely to happen for hundreds of years unless there's a volcanic eruption. Far as I'm concerned the job down here's finished with.'

He nodded towards the bore and the party returned to it bringing the equipment with them. The thought uppermost in each mind hardly needed expressing as helmets were removed and one looked at the other.

'Everything here being completed we're still wondering how to get home, I suppose?' Cliff relaxed at the table and glanced about him upon the grim faces.

'I'm wondering,' Dagman said, 'if Joan's notion of walking home is so crazy as it sounds. After all, people have walked nearly a thousand miles under stress. Maybe we can.'

'We can,' Cliff agreed, 'but what do we do for food and drink? Our rations won't last indefinitely, and certainly they won't stand up to the long period of time needed to cover some eight hundred miles. It would be plain suicide to attempt it.'

'On the other hand we'd die trying to save ourselves,' Blair pointed out, 'which to my mind is preferable to sitting here waiting for extinction.'

'Oxygen wouldn't hold out, either,' Naysmith remarked. 'I'm for stopping here and trying to work something out Dammit, we're not imbeciles. There must be a way!'

The others looked at him not at all happily. Then as his eyes wandered to the steel hawser which had been brought in from the shaft-sealing operation a gleam came into his eyes.

'Suppose,' he said slowly, 'we tried the age-old idea of counterbalanced weights?'

'Meaning what?' Blair asked irritably.

'Find a boulder which by weight is approximately the same as that of the bore. Tie one end of the hawser round the rock and the other to the bore, then arrange some means of tipping the boulder down the mountain face. If we men pushed as the boulder fell it might make up the difference and pull the bore up the escarpment to the tunnel mouth.'

'Possible,' Dagman admitted. 'But what then? The master-bar is smashed to blazes this time. We couldn't start up even if we did reach the tunnel opening.'

'Mmmm — ' Naysmith relaxed again. 'I'd forgotten that.'

'I have an idea,' Joan said slowly. 'Probably it's crazy because I'm not a scientist, but here it is for what it's worth. Why not cast an entirely new master-bar? Make it from some of the metal plates of the bore that you think can be sacrificed. Melt it down.'

'Furnace isn't big enough,' Cliff grunted. 'We need a crucible seven feet long and at least two feet wide for a master-bar. So that washes it up.'

'Here are we in the heart of an inferno, a place where rock and metals boil like milk, and you talk about furnace!' Joan exclaimed. 'I'm surprised at you. As for a crucible, you don't need one. Even I know that metal can be cast in a sand bed mould. It's done very often in iron found-ries. A crucible is not vitally necessary in an emergency.'

'By all the saints, I believe you've got something, Joan!' Blair looked up urgently from moody reflections. 'The fact that you are not a scientist may prove our salvation. You've taken the common-or-garden method whilst we've been thinking in terms of modern blasting and smelt-ing.'

He looked at the other men. 'We could use several of the plates which form the walls between the compartments. They are not of the toughest tungsten steel, but at least they ought to stand up to the sort of pressure we'll need. It won't be excessive once we've got up the escarp-ment face. We could melt the plates by sawing them up into pieces and putting them in the crucible Cliff here used for his molten rock. We could probably do the smelting with our electric furnace, but it would drain the power plant so much it might not be practical. The better way is to smelt the stuff in the chasm outside, using the winch and hawser. The remaining snag is sand for the mould. We haven't any sand at this depth.'

'Soon can have,' Cliff said. 'Sand is only powdered rock. We have flame guns that can destroy rock and reduce it to powder. That powder is sand.'

'Once again you're taking the long way round,' Joan sighed. 'Our bore disintegrated rock into fine sand all the way down from the surface. If we go up to the tunnel on foot we'll find all the sand we want, I think. Residual deposit from the exhaust tubes.'

Cliff snapped his fingers. 'That's it! I really believe Joan has it, gentlemen. Let's get moving. Naysmith, you have a look for sand — and you give him a hand, Dagman. As a geologist you'll know whether it's the sort of stuff we're looking for. You and I, Dr. Blair, will make exact measurements for the master-bar we want.'

'And I sit and twiddle my thumbs?' Joan questioned, at which Cliff glanced at her.

'Aren't many jobs which a woman can do in a case like this, Joan. Unless you want to go with Dagman and Naysmith and see if there's any sand.'

'I'll do that. Anything's better than just sitting around.'

The incentive of something to do, some plan to solve their problem, was enough to get all of them quickly on the move. Very shortly they ventured forth, once again in their helmets, and whilst Cliff and Blair made exact measurements of the required master-bar, Naysmith, Dagman, and Joan slowly went up the cliff face until they had reached the tunnel mouth.

To their delight there was all the sand they could need, not entirely the residue of the bore's disintegrating equipment, but created by the rocks which had been ground to sand-powder by the drill.

'All we need are receptacles to carry the sand away, and that's that,' Naysmith said cheerfully.

The three returned down the escarpment, handed the gladsome news on to Cliff and Blair, and then they rigged up a line by which the receptacles of sand could be lowered from the tunnel mouth to the plateau. Everything they did was with primitive slowness, since they had to rig up what devices they could to overcome the shortage of proper equipment. But with Joan and Naysmith collecting the sand on the plateau and Dagman loading up the receptacles in the tunnel, another hour saw the sand-mould for the metal in its preliminary stages. The rest was up to Dr. Blair, who knew more about moulding metal than anyone else.

The moment he and Cliff had finished their calculations on the size and shape of the bar needed, he went to work on fixing the sand bed as he wanted it. The other menfolk set up the winch on the plateau edge and peered into the smoking, boiling tumult of the volcanic chasm below them.

'Well, we know the hawser's long enough, anyway,' Naysmith remarked, 'because you used it, Cliff.'

'Yes, but there are difficulties,' Cliff told him. 'I simply scooped up molten rock as one would draw water out of a well. In this job we're taking on now we only want the crucible to float in the molten liquid long enough for the heat to melt the metal plates in the crucible. If the crucible goes below the surface of the molten stuff down there, we'll bring up molten rock as well as the metal, and that will adulterate it. We can't afford to do that. As pure metal it stands a chance: adulterated it won't stand any.'

'Which,' Joan said, 'means somebody going down there to be sure what's going on. Somebody who can signal when the metal has melted and who can signal to stop lowering when the crucible is in the right position.'

'That's it.' Cliff looked into the depths. 'Another nice job I've got to do from the look of it.'

'I don't see why,' Joan argued. 'You've already risked your neck sealing that shaft: I don't see why you should have to do this as well.'

'I'll go then,' Naysmith said promptly just forestalling an offer from Dagman.

'Frankly,' Joan said, 'I think this is a job for me. Oh, not because I want to be a heroine or because I like taking my life in my hands — but because it will take you men all your time to haul up the crucible when the metal's melted, and then manhandle it to the sand bed. I'll be dead in that act, so I think my share lies down there.'

'No!' Cliff said flatly. 'I'll throw the whole idea overboard first.'

Joan smiled behind her helmet. 'This isn't just a little matter between you and me, Cliff: it's up to everybody here. Our lives depend on this, remember. You don't have to worry about me. I'll manage all right.'

At that moment Dr. Blair came over. He nodded back to the sand bed.

'That's all fixed. Toughest job will be wangling the crucible so we pour the molten metal accurately. Once that's done the mould I've designed should do the rest.'

'I'm going down this cliff face to keep a check on the crucible,' Joan said with a certain touch of defiance. 'Do you see anything wrong with the idea?'

'Wrong? Why, no, I think it's a very good one. In any case we're all in this together.'

'That settles it then,' Cliff sighed. 'I'd

rather it hadn't to be, but there it is — we'd better get busy seeing what plates we can spare and cut, hadn't we?'

The others nodded, and a return was made to the bore. Some hours later, which included a break for a meal and a rest, the crucible had been duly filled with sawn-up metal, and it took all the strength of the four men to manhandle it outside and across the plateau to the winch. Once they had it fastened to the hawser they spent some time experimenting with the 'swing' to determine how best to overturn the crucible of molten metal when it was withdrawn from the depths. Finally they had it to their liking, and turned to look at Joan in her fireproof suit, a safety line fastened to the belt about her waist.

'Ready?' Cliff asked morosely.

'More than! And don't look so unhappy! If I've got to die I may as well do it being useful. You're far more worried about this than I am, you know.'

Cliff did not say anything more. The safety line was held by Naysmith and himself and for extra safety the end of it was noosed round a rock spur. Then Joan began her descent into the smoking depths, gripping the line with her gloves and pedalling with her feet, much after the fashion of a seeker of seagull's eggs.

To those above she was presently lost to sight in the smoke wreaths. Cliff and Naysmith retained their grip on the rope, paying it out very gradually until at last they received the long-awaited signal from below. Joan had evidently reached a point where she could view the proceedings. And indeed she had. She was perched on a rocky needle that jutted over the molten sea a dozen feet below her. The heat was overpowering and the danger extreme, but she refused to be deterred from her task. Flattened against the rock she waited anxiously for something to happen from above.

After a while the crucible came swinging into view on the end of the hawser. It swung dangerously near to Joan's head, and she ducked swiftly; then it began to lower the remaining distance. She watched it intently, giving a sharp 'Stop!' signal on her lifeline as it reached the molten sea and began to float upon it.

Now was the anxious period, there being no guide as to the approximate heat of the molten sea, and therefore no way of judging how long the metal pieces would take to melt. Joan remained at her task, watching the crucible glow red-hot after a moment or two, then it assumed a phosphorescent quality as the heat mounted still more. Within the crucible the metal pieces began to slide and dissolve slowly like grease in a heated frying pan.

Both to Joan and those above it seemed ages before the melting process was complete, and by this time Joan herself felt ready to melt also. Giddy with heat and the overpowering imprisonment of her fireproof suit and head-helmet, she gave the double signal to those above and then lay flat on her face and waited whilst the crucible was hauled up. She fancied that splashes of the molten metal descended upon her judging from the heavy thumps striking her suit, but the special material kept her unharmed.

She allowed sufficient time to elapse for

those above to empty the crucible into the mould and then began to signal to be hauled up. Presently she found herself sailing into the air, and reached the top of the escarpment about spent from her endeavours. Cliff and Naysmith hauled her to her feet as she stumbled.

'Well, did you manage it?' she panted, her sweat-drenched face eager behind the helmet.

'Uh-huh, thanks to you.' Cliff gripped her bloated shoulders. 'How about you? Feel any the worse?'

'Only a bit weak, and I may as well admit now I was scared to death down there! It's the nearest I've ever been to the gates of Hades — Where's the metal? I want to look at it.'

She went over to where Blair and Dagman were studying the already cooling metal in the sand bed. The shape was plainly that of the master-bar, though very rough in outline.

'We've some time to wait for this,' Blair said, 'so we'd better knock off and take a rest. We certainly need it.'

Once again they trooped into the bore

and closed the airlock door, afterwards ridding themselves of their protective suits and helmets. In fifteen minutes they had all freshened themselves up, and recovered somewhat from their labours.

'That was a pretty near thing,' Blair said soberly. 'The crucible is forged to stand the ultimate in heat, but even at that it came to the very edge of melting. A few minutes longer and we'd have lost the lot. Thanks to your vigilance, Joan, that didn't happen.'

Joan shrugged. 'I saw my duty and I did it — as the old soldier said. Providing the bar cools properly, as it should, what happens then? It'll have to be drilled and finished off, won't it?'

'We've got all that figured out,' Cliff answered. 'We have the tools necessary — a drill, a lathe, shaping mechanisms. Thank heaven we came prepared for most eventualities!'

'There's one thing we have learned,' Dagman reflected, 'and that is that on future journeys of this kind we'd better carry two of everything, the same as a car carries a spare tyre. All future bores must carry a spare master-bar and, if it can be arranged, spare tractor belts too.'

'Carried,' Naysmith agreed, grinning. 'First of all, though, I'd prefer to see the blessed light of day before we work out preventatives.'

Silence, each one musing not too happily; then Joan got to her feet.

'We might as well have another meal and keep our strength up. By that time the metal bar may have cooled. Think so, Dr. Blair?'

He nodded, and Joan turned away to her simple domestic task. The moment the meal was over the party ventured outside again, and to their delight the bar was cold, stained bluish white where the cooling had been faster in some places than in others. Naysmith and Cliff hauled up one end of it, and Blair and Dagman made a careful examination.

'Okay,' Blair said finally. 'Near as I can tell without instruments for critical analysis, this bar is the key to home. The sooner we get busy polishing it off, the better.'

It took the strength of all four men to

carry it to the bore, and here again they had to work under difficulties because the tool chamber was not large enough to take the bar's length. Finally they angled it half into the control room, supporting one end from the roof stanchions with steel cable. Then began the task of lathing and drilling.

It was not a job to complete within an hour, or even several hours. They worked on it until well into the 'night' — according to the chronometer — and then resumed activity after a period of sleep. Altogether it was nearly twenty-four hours before they had the job completed, and then came the vital job of linking up.

So well had they worked to specification, and so accurate had been Dr. Blair's measurements, they were not out by even a single fraction on a single bolt hole. The assembly was neatly and efficiently completed, and when it was over the party looked at each other.

'Now for it,' Blair said. 'We're starting under a handicap by being halfway up a rise to begin with. That throws extra strain on the master-bar.'

'Then why don't we use my original suggestion?' Naysmith questioned. 'Find a rock of similar size as a counterbalancing weight and then we have it. I'm convinced it's worth trying.'

'I think the bar will stand up as it is,' Cliff insisted. 'The counterweight idea is all right in one sense, Naysmith, but very risky in another. It means finding a rock spur as our 'pulley' and if that rock spur should snap under the strain — as it easily might — the rock would be down on top of us. I'm for trying as we are.'

Naysmith shrugged, taking the decision with his usual carefree smile.

'See what you can do with the switchboard, Joan,' Cliff instructed, glancing at her. 'We'll remain here and keep an eye on the bar. Remember, only the merest trickle of power to commence with until we get on the move — '

Joan hurried away and back into the bore, closing the airlock behind her. Presently, she became visible through the main outlook window, her finger and thumb 'O'd' to show she was ready. Cliff signalled back with a wave of his hand, perched with Blair, Dagman, and Naysmith on the plates immediately over the master-bar.

It began to turn slowly, transmitting its power to the tractor belts. The bore resumed its slow crawl up the bumpy face of the cliff, creeping over rocks, flattening into hollows, nosing upwards again exactly like a tank, its powerful drill jutting ready for action if an extra large rock became an obstacle. This did not happen, fortunately, and the men looked at each other with tense faces as, foot by foot, the machine inched its way higher.

'I do believe we're going to do it,' Blair whispered, clasping his hands together tightly as though he were praying. 'For the love of Mike don't die on us now.'

A jolt. The machine dipped dizzily into a deep rock hollow; then it righted itself again. Cliff glanced up towards the rocky cave — the tunnel mouth — towards which they were crawling, and looked away again. Retentively, though, something stuck in his memory, and he looked again. There was something up there which had not been visible before. It looked grey and it seemed to be moving — but that was not the only thing. A mighty rock in front of the greyness was tottering slowly forward —

'Look out!' Cliff yelled hoarsely, and with the desperate urge of self-preservation he leapt for his life, tumbling into the midst of the rocks.

Blair, Naysmith, and Dagman did not have the same length of time in which to grasp the situation. They glanced up in alarm just in time to see a vast boulder bouncing down towards them — It hit the bore with shattering force, crushing the metal plates, snapping the improvised master-bar, whirling the whole contrivance head over heels down the slope and down to the bottom of the escarpment. It halted upside down, its power plant silent.

The din and the dust subsided. Shaking with reaction, Cliff slowly straightened up and looked about him. Up above, dust was clouding everything and there was no sign of that queer moving grey shape he had seen. But he did glimpse the three scientists and just as quickly jerked his face away. There was obviously nothing that could be done for them.

And Joan? He began to race down the slope, tripping over the rocky fragments and finally coming to a sliding standstill. The giant boulder that had caused the damage had vanished, but its track was obvious. It had bowled across the plateau and apparently finished up in the molten canyon beyond. But why? Why? What on earth had dislodged it in the first place? There was surely nothing living at this depth in the Earth? And yet that grey shape had appeared to move . . .

These were the thoughts that chased through Cliff's brain as he hurried down the slope, then, in his anxiety to find out what had happened to Joan he did not speculate any further upon the cause of the disaster. He fully expected to find Joan smashed against one of the walls of the overturned machine, for there were limits to the gyroscopic control of the inner cabin. It was not made to handle a complete somersault of the outer casing.

He fumbled with the airlock and wrenched it open, stumbling to the ceiling of the control room, which was now the floor. Anxiously he looked around him in the still functioning light as he shut the airlock door. Almost immediately he sighted Joan, and he gave a gasp of relief. Something had evidently led her to fasten the safety belt about her waist.

'Thank heaven!' Cliff exclaimed, tugging off his stifling helmet. 'I expected to find you smashed in pieces.'

'What happened?' There was a puzzled look on Joan's face. 'I thought a bomb had gone off! Then the bore started flying round in circles and I finished up like this.'

'No bones broken?' Cliff questioned, raising her so he could unfasten the belt buckle.

'No; but I'm getting cramped swinging up here. Hurry it up!'

Cliff jerked the belt free and she tumbled down into his arms. He set her down and she gave him a troubled look as she pushed back her disordered hair.

'Cliff, what's happened?' Her hand gripped his arm. 'I can tell from your expression something's horribly wrong. The bar broke, didn't it?'

'I'm afraid so, and several of the plates are smashed in. As for our three colleagues — ' Cliff looked away. 'I saw their remains amidst the rocks. They were right in the track of that damnable boulder which hit us.'

'Was that what happened?'

'Yes. A boulder got dislodged somehow and landed right on top of us. I jumped clear. Somehow, Joan, I could swear that that boulder was pushed. It didn't look like an accident.'

'Pushed?' Joan repeated in bewilderment. 'But there isn't any life down here, surely?'

'That's what I told myself, and yet — We'd better take a look at the damage.'

'Yes, I suppose so. And what about Naysmith, and the others? We ought to bury them, oughtn't we? It's horrible to think they have been killed, but even down here we can't just leave them. We can perform some sort of burial ser-vice — '

'No point in it,' Cliff said brusquely,

handing the girl her helmet. 'There's not enough left of them to justify a burial. It's the kind of sight that needs forgetting.'

He opened the airlock and led the way outside, Joan following him. In sombre silence they inspected the upended bore, its tractors facing the mighty cavern roof. At length Cliff crawled underneath the metalwork and examined it carefully with his flashlight.

'Damage to the master-bar isn't as bad as I thought,' he said as Joan peered at him. 'I thought it was smashed, but it isn't that: it's been torn from the bolting union where the power plant shaft connects. I can fix that in about half an hour by casting a fresh bolt.'

'And how much good will that do with the bore upside down? We've no possible means of righting it.'

Cliff squirmed out of the narrow space and then straightened up beside the girl. She looked at him seriously through her helmet glass.

'Y'know, Cliff, I begin to have the feeling that some sort of destiny is preventing us from getting home. This is the second catastrophe, and three valuable lives lost, too!' She glanced up towards the rock face where she pictured the remains of the scientists must be lying, but instead she saw something else, which banished them from her mind. Her convulsive grip on Cliff's arm made him look, too. He felt the short hairs rise on the back of his neck.

There was a grey shape up there in the tunnel mouth. He had not imagined it; and with the offending boulder out of the way the shape slowly took form as it emerged. It was a dinosaur of truly colossal size, its monstrous head moving slowly back and forth as though it were scenting the breeze — or at any rate the nitrogene gases polluting the atmosphere at this depth.

'Dinosaurs down here!' There was incredulity in Cliff's voice. 'It surely isn't possible? The Jurassic region was where we left them — '

'That's a dinosaur, whether or no.' Joan was commencing to back nervously away. 'And what's even more to the point, it's coming down here!'

Cliff whipped his flame gun from his belt and held it in readiness as he saw the vast brute was lurching and stumbling down the slope. His nerves tautened as he realised there was no way of escape for himself and Joan. Behind them was the chasm of molten rock, and to either side the volcanic walls. Joan was conscious of the limitations, too, and ceased her backward movement.

'We can't fight a brute like that with a flame gun,' she panted. 'How about going in the bore and hoping for the best? We might even turn the drill — '

She broke off. All hope of getting into the bore was gone now, for the monster had suddenly seen them both. It emitted a roar that vibrated throughout the colossal cavern and then came thundering down the slope. Cliff watched intently and held his gun. Joan gave a scream and ran, finishing up at the further end of the plateau and crouching down amidst the rocks where she hoped the giant head would not be able to reach her. Cliff glanced, saw what she had done, and raced after her.

With the shattering impact of its eighty odd tons of weight the dinosaur thundered after him, stopping as he jumped down amidst the rocks beside Joan. There, feeling absurdly tiny and completely helpless, they gazed up at the skyscraper of a head as it waved back and forth, the blood-red eyes glittering.

'It's — it's a diplodocus,' Cliff gasped. 'One of the most fearsome of all the prehistoric beasts as well as one of the strongest. How in the name of Satan did it ever get here? Wonder if I can kill it by aiming at the eye?'

He steadied himself to take aim, and the diplodocus seemed to realise what was intended, for it reared up on its hind feet and towered high over the rocks, roaring shatteringly, its forelegs clawing air.

'Wait!' Joan screamed suddenly, clutching Cliff's arm. 'Wait, Cliff, for the love of heaven!'

'Wait? You crazy? I'm going to — '

'Don't fire! I've just thought of something. This may be Herbert!'

Cliff became motionless, stunned with surprise.

'There are no other beasts,' Joan hurried on, as the diplodocus dropped to all four feet again. 'Herbert would be full grown by now. Why this one creature and no others? And he was a dinosaur!'

'Lord!' Cliff felt suddenly weak in the knees.

Joan scrambled up, convinced of the rightness of her theory. In spite of Cliff trying to stop her she scrambled up on to the higher rocks and waved her arms at the mighty brute watching her intently.

'Herbert!' she cried hoarsely, turning her microphone amplifier to maximum. 'Herbert! Stop being playful!'

This was a command she had used often enough in the days of Herbert's infancy — and to her aching relief the diplodocus gave a stupendous bellow. It was not fury or frustration, but sheer delight. It began to caper playfully, setting the ground quaking with its movements.

'By all that's queer, it is Herbert!' Cliff climbed to Joan's side and stood watching the monster's antics. 'But how in the world has it managed to follow us?'

'Don't ask me! How do some ordinary

animals find their way home right across a continent, to somebody they love? That is an animal instinct we can't explain. The fact remains that good old Herbert has followed us down here for nearly a thousand miles. He could, you know,' Joan went on eagerly. 'We only made the journey slowly, and we've been here some time, too. He must have been close behind all the time. Maybe he got our scent, or used a sixth sense, or something. Like a cat that has lost its owner.'

'But food and drink!'

'Didn't Naysmith say that the prehistoric animals can go for days and weeks with stored up water and food? Like a camel? That's what must have happened here.'

There seemed no longer any doubt that the vast carnivore had indeed followed the two whom it had come to love, had pursued them right down here to the core of the world. And now — ?

'Herbert,' Cliff said slowly, putting his gun away, 'is going to be our salvation! He can turn the bore over! And if need be he can shove it up the slope if we can train him! Unfortunate — in fact tragic — that he wiped out Blair, Dagman, and Naysmith, but here's his chance to even things up.'

He stepped down from the rock and shouted to the monster as it careered like some colossal dog around the cavern, flinging aside huge boulders by the flicking of its tail.

'Herbert, come here!' Cliff commanded, and to his satisfaction the diplodocus, slowing up, came lumbering forward. If any further proof of its identity were needed, its tongue came down to lick Cliff's face. Fortunately for him his helmet saved him from getting seared by that long, tearing file of flesh.

'There's another thing, too,' Joan said. 'Whilst he's down here he can't be propagating more monsters — Or does that matter? The failure of nitrogene will kill the rest of them anyway.'

Cliff was not listening very attentively. He was bawling orders to the carnivore and thereby started on the long, tedious task of drilling into its slow-moving brain exactly what was required of it. It would probably take a long time, but it was a way out — the only way out.

★   ★   ★

Though Herbert apparently had the power of regurgitation and for nearly another week kept himself fed and mysteriously slaked his thirst, there came a time when his inner supply ran out, Cliff did the only thing possible. He used the meat rations that had been intended for the three scientists, and fed them to Herbert instead. Small fare, as was the mediocre supply of water, but it seemed enough to keep the giant going. His physical discomforts seemed to be compensated by the fact that he had found the two tiny beings who had showered kindness upon him in his 'cub' days. And, though inherently stupid, he did struggle hard to assimilate the orders that Cliff ceaselessly dinned into him.

Until at last it dawned upon him what was required. With one shove of his gargantuan head he tipped the bore right side up and was rewarded with four cans of pressed beef, the tin of which he crushed in his vice-like jaws and spat out afterwards.

Having got this far the rest was not difficult. Cliff had had the new bolting gear made for some time, and with the bore now the right way up he had no difficulty in reaffixing the master-bar. The matter of the plates was less simple. It demanded he worked from the inside with a sledgehammer, and weld up any fractures. Not that there were any in the inner casing, otherwise the interior atmosphere of the vessel would have been polluted long before.

'Does this mean,' Joan asked, when the master-bar had been fixed and tested, 'that we can make an effort to go home at last?'

'It does, providing Herbert sufficiently understands orders to push the bore from behind. I think he does: I've given him a good drubbing. Anyhow, you take the controls and I'll work on Herbert from the outside until we get to the tunnel.'

'Right!' Joan settled herself in the driving seat and buckled the safety belt.

Cliff put on his helmet and went to the exterior, standing on the summit of the bore's outer case.

'Here, Herbert!' he yelled, and the diplocodus came over from the far side of the cavern.

'Push!' Cliff instructed, but he had to wait nearly half an hour before the brute understood to ram its titanic head at the back of the bore. The fact that it found the bore a hard thing to move was all to the good: it made him push all the harder. This fact, with Joan carefully controlling the power plant, was sufficient to force the machine gradually up the escarpment, Herbert's mighty legs straining with all their power.

So at last to the top of the long rise. The bore tipped its nose down and was facing the tunnel. Here it stopped, positioned ready for the journey — the long, wearisome journey — back home. The airlock opened and Joan, helmeted, appeared.

'What about Herbert?' she questioned. 'We can't leave him here — and yet we don't want him above. Nor do we want him to rejoin the brutes in the Jurassic region.'

'I dunno,' Cliff muttered, descending from the bore's summit to her side. 'He'll have to follow us and maybe tire himself out, or something. We can't kill him, and we wouldn't if we could. Anymore than we would a much-loved pet. Let's be on our way.'

Mutually they dropped the subject and returned to the bore's interior, Cliff this time taking the controls. He drove steadily along the tunnel that the down journey had created, the depth gauge slowly reversing as the miles were covered.

And to the rear there plodded the faithful Herbert just about able to keep up with the bore's speed and also just having enough room to progress. And still the homeward-bound two did not know what to do about him.

They had their answer on the third 'day' of the return trip. Part of the rocky tunnel had apparently collapsed and it demanded the drill for them to get through it. They only just succeeded when the rocks fell again behind them. After that they did not see Herbert again. Evidently even his giant strength had not proven up to breaking the barrier.

'I shall always remember him, sort of sadly,' Joan muttered, staring into the searchlighted depths ahead. 'Prehistoric he may have been, but he had domestic instincts at heart.'

'He was, and is, a thing of the past,' Cliff replied, and that seemed to sum up the issue from all directions.

THE END

We do hope that you have enjoyed reading this large print book.

Did you know that all of our titles are available for purchase?

We publish a wide range of high quality large print books including:
Romances, Mysteries, Classics
General Fiction
Non Fiction and Westerns

Special interest titles available in large print are:
The Little Oxford Dictionary
Music Book, Song Book
Hymn Book, Service Book

Also available from us courtesy of Oxford University Press:
Young Readers' Dictionary
(large print edition)
Young Readers' Thesaurus
(large print edition)

For further information or a free brochure, please contact us at:
Ulverscroft Large Print Books Ltd.,
The Green, Bradgate Road, Anstey,
Leicester, LE7 7FU, England.
Tel: (00 44) 0116 236 4325
Fax: (00 44) 0116 234 0205

DR. MORELLE ELUCIDATES

Ernest Dudley

Dr. Morelle expounds on seven puzzling cases in his inimitable manner. For *The Case of the Man Who Was Too Clever*, the doctor and his assistant Miss Frayle investigate the murder of an actress, whose dying screams are the clue to her death. Whilst in *The Case of the Clever Dog*, a murder is committed in the doctor's presence, but man's best friend is the clue in finding the killer . . .

THE G-BOMB

John Russell Fearn

The cleverest man on Earth, Jonas Glebe, becomes the unwitting tool of a baleful intelligence. His invention, the G-Bomb, should bring riches to himself and his daughter Margaret — instead it brings death and a deadly threat to mankind . . . Val Turner knows the danger, but he's imprisoned — framed for Margaret's murder. His release comes too late to prevent the cataclysm engulfing the world. But fate decrees that he saves a strange little man from drowning, and thereby changes destiny . . .

THE VANISHING MAN

Sydney J. Bounds

Popular novelist and secret agent Alec Black is on an undercover mission on Mars. The Martian colonists are preparing for a major offensive against earth and someone is stirring up war-fever. Black must try to prevent it, or the whole system will be engulfed in atomic war. When Black finds himself shadowed by a man who, when confronted, vanishes into thin air, his investigation turns into his strangest case and very soon he's plunged into a dimension of horror . . .

TOYMAN

E. C. Tubb

Space-wanderer Earl Dumarest is on the planet Toy, hoping he'll get information on the whereabouts of Earth, his lost home world. But nothing is given freely there and he must fight in the Toy Games to gain the information he needs. He's forced to be like a tin soldier in a vast nursery with a spoiled child in command — but there's nothing playful about the Games on Toy. Everything is only too real: pain, wounds, blood — and death . . .